the_way_the_hen_kicks

the_way_the_hen_kicks

Lars Guthorm Kavli

YouCaxton Publications

Oxford & Shrewsbury

<

/>

the_way_the_hen_kicks

/computing_facility_4/final_simulations/
january_27021

/the_fall

Started at Tue Sep 12 03:35:43 27020

Command line was: ./henkick_1258 --out-dir=store/
final_rebuild --out-postfix=arx_run_0_no_clean
--creat-sigma=10 --no-plot --save-plot --kwg-
base=hk_kwg_9.db --drives-list=drives.txt --drive-
idx=97

Version tag 3.12.1.1258, built Tue Sep 12 03:35:40
27020

Job ID is: 182798, 1024 instances allocated

VC hash: 7f5eb4bc96bc

parsing recovered files at /store/recovery/drvX5T

<scale_and_perspective

The Greater London Assembly. A retro-futuristic anachronism. The way one thought the future would look like in the 1950s. A building so impractical it needed cleaning every day. All its surfaces either slanting outwards or inwards, either gathering dust or dropping water onto the heads of passers-by. It had a cleaning staff of about a hundred (the men outside, the women inside, mostly the division went). The freestanding structure was surrounded by an intricate surface of narrow slabs of black stone stretching many hundred metres towards Shad Thames and equally far towards London Bridge. Every day this surface was tended to by an armada of cleaning vehicles that moved ever so slowly, side by side, slightly overlapping the other's trajectory.

Looking at the building from up close was like gorging on an economy-bag of salt and vinegar crisps, a litre and a half of Cherry Coke, a dozen sugar coated donuts, a full tray of homemade lasagne, a jumbo tub of Häagen-Dazs (Cookies and Cream), all in one sitting. Glass upon glass upon more glass, smoked and blue-stained and polished, brushed steel in any shape you could imagine, mostly long and slender and elegant, entrances with hushed rotating doors and blood-red carpets like streams of strawberry sauce. The GLA *More London* complex was a glass-fest, a steel and polished stone party to outdo all such parties – forever. The building mind go... **[syntax error]**

/>

<consulting

As Communications Adviser to the GLA, Bjørn was sitting
in the Mayor's office admiring the pastoral oil paintings,
waiting for the Mayor to return from a charity event. It
was a Saturday afternoon. On the table lay a warm copy
of a report he'd just finished writing, entitled *Digital
Communication and The Future of Political Legitimacy*.
Bjørn was not exactly pleased with it – knew he could've put
in a few more hours, cleaned up a few sentences, actually
whole paragraphs, come to think of it, rewritten the whole
thing, though he'd already done that five times. The stats
were not necessarily all that relevant; the argumentation
cribbed from online sources pretty much anyone could've
looked up. The thing would probably never be read anyway,
so why even bother being nervous about it? Though he was.

The sunlight entering the Mayor's office made millions of microscopic pieces of dust appear to move through the room in a uniform slow motion, the same kind of slow motion Bjørn was experiencing in his head, a thick sense of something he couldn't really name, something that came up from an unsettled feeling in his abdomen, a pressure, or maybe actually a vacuum, something that made it difficult to breathe. The slim-fit shirt clung uncomfortably to his upper body, chafing the armpits. He breathed into his palm to check if his breath was OK. He couldn't tell. He needed the toilet but didn't want to leave in case the Mayor should come back when he was out. The light coming through the newly cleaned windows fell warmly on the expensive furniture, made visible the pores of the tanned leather, gleamed in the chrome legs of the Mayor's gigantic desk. A thick brown woollen blanket lay folded across the leather-couch's armrest. The Arcadian-themed oil paintings hung heavily on the wall to the right of the couch, above the reach of the sun.

"Bjørn...? What are you doing here?"

The Mayor steamed into the room, followed by three surprisingly baby-faced men, all wearing the same type stonewashed jeans, identical black hoodies and white sneakers of brand unknown.

"Mr. Mayor, you wanted this..."

Bjørn got up, attempted a smile and pointed to the report on the table.

"Did I...?"

The Mayor was checking his phone while talking. The three young men stood bad-postured, shoulders slouching forward, their hands in their hoodies' front pockets, obscuring the painting of the large crumbling folly. They looked bored. Uninterested. Like something mass-produced, something ignorant, and yet – arrogant?

"Since you're here. I'd like you to meet..."

The Mayor was still checking his phone while talking. Then he looked up as if he'd surprised himself with an odd thought.

"Our new consultants."

"...?"

"Ah... Bjørn."

The Mayor came towards him with his left arm extended to give him a pat on the shoulder.

"They're helping us consolidate our future scenario planning. Giving us some inspiration. A younger perspective. You see?"

"Oh."

"We're just about to go over a few of these now. Actually, do you say scenaria?"

"I don't know. Scenarios I think."

"In any case. I need help with this speech. It's due Monday."

He fished out a memory stick shaped like a piece of Lego from his trouser pocket and dangled it in the air, his other arm still around Bjørn's shoulder. A smell of musky cologne and halitosis hung about them.

Bjørn looked at his watch: 6:13 p.m. He looked at his report on the table. The three young consultants, if that's what they were, were looking at nothing in particular. Their bored expressions like the faint sound of an alarm ringing.

"Sure," he said. "Glad I can help."

He could do with the money. The GLA paid overtime on Sundays. These were one of the few perks a civil servant ever saw.

"That's the spirit."

The Mayor took him aside.

"I'll make it worth your while. And by the way, you might have to come with me..."

The Mayor looked over at the young consultants.

"To where was it again? Greenland?"

One of them nodded.

"Yes. So to Greenland. Next week?"

"OK."

Bjørn kept nodding as the Mayor returned to his adolescent guests who followed him over to his desk.

The light, coming in past the Shard, all the way from the sun, was still entering the Mayor's office with its precise quality, seemed somehow intent on illuminating the meaning of something Bjørn couldn't quite put his mind's finger on. Something important it felt like he'd just forgotten. Something that had to do with...? No. He couldn't remember. He closed the glass door behind him. What could it have been? It made him increasingly nervous not being able to recall this something that felt like it was so important.

/>

<greenland

Outside the large floor-to-ceiling hotel room window a wind was blowing but you couldn't hear it, you could only see the effects. The building was too well insulated, the windows triple-glazed. A selection of small rubbish and leaves and dust and gravel was swirling around, caught in a mini-tornado on the parking lot. Now and then a stronger lateral gust would shift the whirlwind's position radically, from close to the hotel entrance to down by the exit onto the main road, and then over to by the recycling container next to the local supermarket. It seemed like all the trash-content was intact with each displacement. Beyond the main road, which was a narrow two-laner with no separating line, lay the ocean, restless, dark blue, almost a dirty cobalt. Marshmallows of white spray topped each wave, endlessly disappearing and reforming. It might as well have been the same wave, the same white foamy top each time.

Bjørn felt hung-over. Lethargic. The tiny hotel room was too stuffy. There was too much sweat in the air, too much young testosterone. The pimple-faced consultant who called himself Yaric covered his eyes dramatically in disbelief at the Mayor's sudden reluctance to respond, to say anything at all. They'd been over the same ground five times in the last hour.

"But Mr. Mayor. What kind of snow is you have planned for all this equipments?"

His voice broke into a peeping, rasping falsetto.

"It never snow in London, you know that... You remember discussion last week?"

The Mayor's Malibu-blond secretary Kirsty looked over at the Mayor who looked with an empty expression at Bjørn, who in turn looked at Stefan, as he called himself, before he looked over at Yaric who kept covering his eyes and leaning his head backwards (absurdly far) in his attempt to impress upon the Mayor the futility of the counter-argument: that he shouldn't sell them the city's snow-removal equipment, now that he'd come all this way.

Yaric finally lifted his hand from his face and leaned forward. He looked at Bjørn and the Mayor with the cold glance of a child used to getting its way.

"Come on, eh, Bjørn? Mr. Mayor…? Do we have to play hards?"

The Mayor scratched his head behind his right ear and pulled a distracted grimace as he kept looking down at his feet, saying nothing. Kirsty's eyes went like needy puppies between the other four in the room, who all ignored her. Bjørn studied the colourful pattern of the bedspread as it disappeared underneath the pillows covered in a similar pattern. Then he looked at the pay-TV menu perched on top of the TV. It was encased in hard translucent plastic. There was an image of a woman in her underwear on the right side and on the other was James Bond in his tuxedo, both hands in his trouser pockets, as if he was casually taking a break, off-screen.

Yaric and Stefan got up from their seats and stood where the little hotel room's corridor started, blocking a quick trip to the toilet, which both the Mayor and Bjørn needed (but not if it meant passing the two youngsters). The third unnamed consultant who'd picked them up at the airport was waiting in the lobby. Desperately attractive, Kirsty smiled at everyone in a slow panning movement of the head but none of them acknowledged the smile.

"Mr. Mayor, look this… Look here."

Yaric, trying a softer but overbearing and precocious tone all the same, plunged his hairless hand into the bag hanging around his neck, a bag sporting a very conspicuous Microsoft logo.

"This is statistics report made in Ottawa by fellow scientist students."

He took out a spiral-spined document, its pages worn at the edges. He glanced at it, nodded in a satisfied way to himself and held it out to the Mayor. The Mayor looked at Bjørn. Bjørn looked at the Mayor. Yaric looked at both of them and held the document in front of Bjørn, or rather, he waved it back and forth before he patted him on the arm with it and smiled.

"Lookeh Bjørn. This is as good as Magnus Carta, OK? Like the constitution of England my friend. Solids. No needs to worry."

Bjørn accepted the document reluctantly and looked at the first few pages. It was written in Cyrillic. The front-page formatting reminded him of a screenplay, the title typed in Courier bold, centre aligned, mid-page, its meaning completely inaccessible to him. There was an image grabbed from an online map on page two. It was London. It had a big emoticon sun placed in the corner of Epping Forest. It smiled with closed eyes and radiated yellow and warm-looking rays.

He flipped further. On each left-hand page was a graph dotted with an intense amount of data, illegible, incomprehensible at a glance (and probably after prolonged study). They looked like the front-lights of a car smeared with gnats, dense, uncorrelatable. On the facing right-hand page was what Bjørn assumed to be the graph's explanatory text, the document's running argument. Bjørn could make out a few formulas, but their meaning lay far beyond his mathematical ability. He kept flipping through the pages as though doing so the text would somehow reveal its meaning, like shaking a plant to release its seeds. He did it just as much to avoid looking up. The document was obviously bogus, shoddy as homework done on the morning of class. It was laughable, but there it was, and there they were, in a hotel room in Greenland.

On the last page, having turned to it six times, Bjørn couldn't avoid seeing the name of the alleged publishing body, not the Université d'Ottawa, as Yaric had claimed, but the Porter School of Environmental Studies, Tel Aviv University, Israel. Though that noted, the label seemed photocopied from another book or report. And that photo-copying effect was what was so peculiar about the graphs as well; the dense spattering of gnats between the X and the Y-axis, like the grain that appeared on a page that carried the copy of an original, copied hundreds of times over, the dust inside the copy machine settling all over the page, the contrast turned up as the original copy was losing darkness, the dust turning into specks with their own secret meaning.

He was sure he would throw up. He directed all his efforts at suppressing the matter he could feel growing from his stomach into his oesophagus. He handed the thing back to Yaric, who threw it on the bed. The Mayor looked at Bjørn quizzically, but Bjørn couldn't meet his eyes. Instead he looked at Stefan who was handing Yaric what he assumed was the contract.

"Mr. Mayor, Sir, please, here is paperswork..."
/>

<species

Back in his hotel room Bjørn took a five-minute leak, leaning with one hand against the tiled wall above the toilet. When he was done he avoided looking at himself in the large mirror over the washbasin. He closed the door to the toilet, removed his shoes and suit-pants, his tie, socks and wristwatch and crept under the tightly fitted duvet, ignoring to loosen it at the foot-end. With his shirt still on he lay without moving, looking at the massive old-style TV on the monumental TV-stand, the wooden desk and mini-bar, trying to hear the wind blowing against the wooden wall and the triple-glazed windows to his left. It was three in the afternoon. The curtains were open and the room was alternately very bright or quite dark as the sun appeared or disappeared behind the shifting cover of clouds. He could hear water running in pipes, someone talking faintly down the corridor. He closed his eyes but opened them again immediately. He looked through the large floor-to-ceiling windows. The low clouds were rushing silently across a rocky outcropping above the small beach, on the other side of the two-laner that ran before the hotel. He could see the waves relentlessly falling onto the shore, one retreating as fast as a new one arrived, the foam blowing across the beach, some shrub, then onto the road. A torn plastic bag flew rapidly past. A single white car appeared where the two-laner took a right-turn around the rocks, its headlights on. It drove past the recycling container at the bottom of the supermarket's parking lot and out of view to the left. The wind seemed to have momentarily calmed down, or he couldn't really tell, but it felt that way. Bjørn looked at the colourful bedspread covering his body. He looked at the TV beyond the lump his feet made and saw the room reflected convexly in the glass. Among the pillows he couldn't see his own face in the reflection. He grabbed the remote from the bedside table and turned on the TV.

He switched off the hotel information channel – flipped past the local channels, past the 24-hour news on CNN and BBC, past the shopping channels, past the daytime Australian soaps on an infinite run, a dart-game on Eurosport, past a localised version of MTV, the numerous Disney channels, what looked like a home and gardening channel, past Arte (in French), past Hallmark, adverts for insurance and detergent, past the adult pay-per-view, Russia Today, the weather-channel, the poker-channel, stopping at Discovery, which caught his attention.

On screen a large feline was running after a rabbit, the rabbit escaping to safety in amongst some boulders. According to the voice-over, the adolescent Iberian lynx would gradually perfect its hunting ability over the coming summer, which was not only a question of its own survival, but that of its species. It was the most critically endangered of all feline species, forced to share its shrinking habitat with farmers, in between a growing matrix of motorways, sprawling housing and small-scale industry, in the south-western highlands of Spain.

The shifting light from the outside was making it hard to see the screen clearly but Bjørn didn't want to draw the curtains. Instead he sat up a little and placed another pillow at his back.

A female adult lynx was shown, filmed at night with infrared technology, struggling to find its way past wire-fencing and illegal traps laid out by local goat farmers. The animal's eyes lit up green and ghost-like in the grainy footage, probably made more ethereal by the sheen in the old TV's rounded screen. Then it slinked away into the darkness it had appeared from.

According to recent conservationist research there were a minimum of 84 and a maximum of 134 adult Iberian lynxes left in the wild, divided across two separate breeding populations. And despite strong efforts, both by the Spanish government and international NGOs, the Iberian lynx would probably be extinct in the wild within ten to fifteen years. The tone of the documentary was solemn. The end-credits started rolling over a view of a lone member of the species surveying the green and brown landscape from the top of a rock. It was filmed in silhouette and the camera flare made the TV look golden and beautiful in the dull hotel room. Before the credits were done the adverts came on and Bjørn turned the TV off.

The wind had picked up again it seemed, or at least it felt that way. The sky had grown a uniform dark grey and the daylight seemed to be slipping. He threw the remote on the floor, got to his feet and walked over to the window. He realised he would be visible like that, from the road, the parking lot, barelegged, only his wrinkled shirt-tails coming down his thighs. Another lone car came around the bend where the two-laner took a right-turn, its headlights barely illuminating the road ahead of it. It turned into the hotel's parking lot and came to a halt. But no one stepped out. At least Bjørn couldn't see anyone doing so in the growing twilight.

</>

<exploitation

Later that evening. The hotel-bar was dark in a rock 'n' roll kind of way. Glasses were clinking. Someone was laughing hard, down by the entrance. Peanuts were rattled around in shallow bowls. The bartender looked bored. The Mayor leant drunkenly over the low glass table, the turquoise puff underneath him threatening desertion, his gaze swimming in and out of focus, his left hand clutching a packet of antacids. He swallowed some more champagne and grinned before he continued.

"As I said. When you have something, you have to exploit it. You have to make money with it. Otherwise it's no good. It's wasted. See what I mean?"

Bjørn took a long sip from his tall G&T, the ice cubes cooling his upper lip. He looked at the Mayor before he looked at Yaric and Stefan, the two Canadian boys, who really were Russian but somehow also Israeli. They hadn't said much at all, not after securing the signature. Their third companion was gone, or perhaps waiting somewhere to make sure things panned out OK. The Mayor's secretary Kirsty was looking down at her lap so Bjørn looked at her too. He found her hopelessly attractive.

The Mayor ordered another bottle of champagne, the fourth by Bjørn's count.

"That's how I feel anyway, it's my working metaphor. If you have something. If you don't exploit it, then you've fucked up. Not grasped the potential in you or in what you have, what you've come across. And run with it. You really have. Fucked up."

The champagne arrived in a bucket and The Mayor stopped talking in order to dry the bottle, pop an antacid, pour a glass and take a big sip.

"That's how I understand you boys as well. Right? From what you've said. Right? Boys?"

The two teenagers, still dressed in the same casual outfits of a week ago, barely nodded, having regained their uninterested attitude.

"Right, so we all have something then. We come into positions. And possessions. Where and with which. We can make a difference. All of us. Right? Right? At some point in our lives. That's my theory. Anyway. And. That's when you either follow your path, right? As with Aristotle. When you bring your potential to its fulfilment. Right? Or you don't. And you're blind. To what you really are. Excuse me. You don't know yourself. Right Bjørn? You agree with that?"

There was too much noise in the bar – music, chatter, glasses clinking, laughter – so Bjørn hadn't really heard what the Mayor had been saying, but he nodded anyway.

"Right. So. When."

The Mayor sat up and tried to talk over his acid-reflux. "So."

He breathed hard, as if he was squeezing out a big one in the other end. The champagne was not helping. He poured another glass.

"This is all. We have. To do."

The two multi-national youngsters looked at the Mayor and urged him on by not saying anything. Kirsty was looking down and no one was looking at her. She was wearing a perfect dress for the occasion. The nail polish immaculate. Her shoes nicely heeled. She was smoking a smokeless so didn't have to look up to avert the smoke. She was reflecting on what the Mayor had just said. It rang true somehow. Like there was a law of nature like that. But it also rang horribly wrong, because if? If she used what she had, and knew it, and planned it, then? Then she was lost to that. Then it was forever that. Then there was no relaxing or just taking it easy and letting things float on and by and having a good time. No. Then it was always on. Always potentially exploiting the potential. Endlessly. Whereas if she didn't use or exploit what she had, then, she might be free?

She'd felt trapped by her beauty as a girl. She still felt that way now, how she *was* trapped, how nobody dared to look at her. Was it her mother's fault? Pushing her to exploit her looks? Mother earth? The way things went?

"Things change. And."

The Mayor was still struggling with his heartburn but forced himself onwards. His voice went lower, sort of whisper-like.

"If you don't see the angle. Coming. Excuse me."

He coughed to see if that would help.

"The potential. The way things. Will move. Then. Right? Am I right?"

His face was turning dark red.

Yaric and Stefan nodded and slurped some Cherry Coke through the straws they'd asked for, their glasses filled to the rim with crushed Greenland glacier ice. Bjørn had the feeling he could either get smashed or go to bed. It didn't matter. Either way. He looked up at the bar's ceiling but couldn't see it in the darkness. He imagined they were sitting outside but just didn't know it. He imagined the stars above and satellites flying glowing through the pattern of light. A real calmness came over him. What did it matter? What was the worst that could happen? And if the worst happened? So what? It didn't matter. He didn't care. He lowered his gaze from the ceiling he couldn't see and panned it around the room. Everything was so beautiful. All of it was just as nature had intended, or rather, how it turned out after millions and millions of years. And this was it. The red mahogany bar. The light falling on it. The way people were dressed. The glasses filled with wonderful magical liquid that made men and women smile and kiss and want to fuck each other. Make babies. That was it! There was nothing else. He chuckled. Almost laughed. Maybe he'd try to talk to Kirsty later? Yes. Maybe he finally would. He lifted his arm and let it fall onto the chair's armrest.

/>

/snowing

Started at Wed Sep 13 03:29:36 27020

Command line was: ./henkick_1259 --out-dir=store/
final_rebuild --out-postfix=arx_run_0_no_clean
--creat-sigma=10 --no-plot --save-plot --kwg-
base=hk_kwg_9.db --drives-list=drives.txt --drive-
idx=98

Version tag 3.12.1.1259, built Wed Sep 13 03:29:33
27020

Job ID is: 146942, 1066 instances allocated

VC hash: 3b7fa3dc81ae

parsing recovered files at /store/recovery/drvY9L

At a relatively modest height above London new snowflakes were continuously forming around gazillion specs of dust. First an afterthought of water condensing, then freezing, each crystallizing into a unique shape. Then they fell to earth, one after another, in uncountable numbers, pulled down by the subtle persistence of gravity, with really no space between them at all, across the whole city. A continuous slow curtain-fall of white. Snow falling heavily over Leicester Square and Green Park. Thick and watery over Victoria Station and the British Museum. Densely over rows and rows of houses in the suburbs. Above the London Eye and the Emirates Stadium. Fluffy and light over Harrods and Crystal Palace. Over Royal Albert Hall and The Hackney Empire. Slowly over Cutty Sark and the Houses of Parliament. Softly over kebab shops and Starbuckses. Over roundabouts and tube-entrances, churches and parking lots. Over the Thames from Kemble to Sheerness. Over the surfaces of the north London reservoirs. Over Epping Forest. Over shopping malls and multiplex cinemas. Snow coming down evenly and persistently over care-homes for the elderly, job centres and prisons. Over kindergartens and playgrounds. Over office blocks and council estates. Through all kinds of frequency waves, through light emitted from lamp-posts and giant advertising screens. Through laser-beams pointed skywards. A dense snowfall. Uniformly white it came down from the sky. Nauseating. Hypnotic.

And where the individual snow-crystals met the ground or any other surface they started piling up fast. Their infinitely varied shapes interlocking. On handrails and fences, rooftops and bus-shelters, on the branches of trees, on baldachins outside 'gentlemen's clubs', on restaurant awnings, a growing layer of pristine snow, settling, compacting. It landed on people's shoulders, was brushed out of hair. Filled up satellite dishes. Weighed down and bent TV antennae. It covered pavements, the tops of gravestones, cycling-paths, the bottoms of barges, ventilation pipes, traffic lights, the heads of statues. Its increasing weight exerted a growing pressure, unplanned-for by architects and engineers.

Meteorological updates were sent by the minute to radio and TV stations and websites needing such info. Airport control towers were told to go to a higher degree of alertness. Colour orange. The first trains were already stalling mid-track, being abandoned through the front and rear. The Transport for London HQ motherboard had tallied seventy-seven bus-crashes since the first snowflakes had been reported. Natives were running for cover. Even the more weather-hardened immigrants were making a dash for it – the Polish and the Russians; the Swedes and the Canadians; the Icelandic; the few Greenlanders, the Norwegians. Southern-hemisphere-heeding folks were long since at home, turning up heaters and boiling water for cups of tea with much milk and much sugar, preparing to sensibly wait it out. On the M25, traffic had totally stopped. Cars stood bumper-to-bumper with headlights on as far as you could see, damp rising from their hoods, wet exhaust billowing out behind them. From above, through the snowflakes, the chain of light and smoke looked like a ring of lava erupting, welling out from the earth's core.

People sitting in their cars, in ones or twos, felt a rising sense of worry, a restlessness taking hold, as they couldn't move, didn't know what to do. Couples started arguing about nothing at all. Radio and TV stations disrupted their normal schedule. DJs and announcers were trying as best they could to deliver the minute-by-minute forecasts with a sense of calm, though most were failing and regrettably adding to the mounting sense of tension. It seemed even meteorological devices were being hit directly, knocked out of use, the snow too heavy.

In London's many parks it was suddenly so quiet you could hear your own breath. On Hampstead Heath no one was about. Crows had gathered in large trees and were sitting still. A few sparrows shuttled to and fro their nests, trying to gather the last of what they could find to eat. Cats and dogs were virtually gone from the surrounding streets, the few still about more wild than tame, curiously walking from underneath cars to underneath hedges, their tracks quickly covering over, sniffing the air as if there was something entirely new about it.

/>

<dizzying

Bjørn had woken early, fifteen minutes before the alarm, and had felt unusually rested. He'd thought about the day ahead. None of the scheduled appointments had promised a slog or a struggle. A few sunrays had peeked through the blinds. He'd realised he was actually looking forward to the day, something he hadn't done in a long while. He'd even managed to lose some weight, having kept up a regular gym-routine for the last four months. He'd been looking forward to the weekly breakfast briefing with the press. There would be coffee, pastries, water from large jugs. A kind of understated quality he liked. He'd anticipated the effect his new tartan-patterned shirt would have. Not a traditional choice but he'd hoped a good one. Its slim-fit cut made him look younger than he was, now that his waist was under some kind of control again. He'd felt the day had promise. A sense of quiet achievement. Of things being in their place once more. Ordered according to his liking.

Around 4 p.m. it had grown overcast, quickly, and the wind had picked up, and within minutes the sky had been dense with fog. Two hours later, as Bjørn had walked home across Tower Bridge, a heavy rain had started falling, soaking his clothes through to his skin, followed by painful hail-showers. By early evening, standing behind the apartment's balcony glass-doors, Bjørn had observed the first snowflakes swirling playfully through the air. And within an hour the surface of the balcony had been covered with a ten-centimetre carpet of snow. He'd remained standing, more or less motionless, seeing the snowfall intensify, for what must've been hours. His two flat-sharers were not at home. He'd not turned on the lights. Looking up he could see no end to the matrix of crystals falling. He had a sense of being in a continuum of snow. Just like you were in a continuum of water under water, or in a continuum of air when you walked about on a normal day. The snow fell with that kind of infinite symmetry and order, all the flakes in a seemingly equal distance from each other, moving at a uniform speed in one direction with no lateral shift. Mesmerising. Dizzying.

Standing almost paralyzed, looking into the snow, he felt a particular memory emerging from his childhood in Norway. It had been stored in him for so long. Now it appeared complete before his inner projector.

He could've been fourteen. He was sitting with three friends at one of the tables provided for its customers by the local Shell station. It was autumn. A red and yellow light came down from the giant logo on top of the tall freestanding structure next to them. The same yellow and red light came down from the Perspex panes running along the edge of the tanking area's elevated roof. They were eating sweets purchased from the station. Synthetic tangy bars, multicoloured wine-gums, drops in all kinds of shapes and inventive packaging. It had made him salivate intensely, he now remembered. Around the light emitted from the station and the streetlights that ran along the passing road, there was an encroaching autumn darkness. Silhouettes of treetops moved without a sound up against the last faint remains of the sunset, towards the west. Every time a car had come to tank, the smell of petrol or diesel had filled the air.

He remembered he'd been hoping for something exciting to happen that evening. For some of the girls they knew from school to come by and talk to them. At the same time he remembered sensing an eerie force lurking at the edge of the artificial light, a latent threat – that this something, whatever it was, had the power to upset everything. To stop him from grasping what felt like it could be his.

He realised the memory was brought on by watching the freshly falling snow. For it had started snowing that evening as well, so long ago, the first snow of autumn, as Bjørn had walked home on his own.

/>

<the_mayor

From the Mayor of London's office atop the GLA the sky looked like a uniform white emptiness, even though it was late evening. The Mayor stood with his head propped against the row of windows facing the already slushy river. His breath appeared on the glass – then disappeared before it appeared again. It had been snowing for three hours solid.

The Mayor wasn't a bad man, or a bad person; at least he didn't feel he was one. Some people had even told him he had a good heart. But he'd made that deal with Yaric and Stefan and whatever that other boy was called. It was true. He'd sold all the snow-removal equipment the city had ever owned, down to the last fucking shovel. Did that mean his efforts as a politician over a long career were nothing worth? Had he simply erased every other good deed by signing that piece of paper? By giving in to their ridiculous demands? He felt it couldn't be so. That it was too harsh if it was true. But he realised it might be.

Standing by the slanting windows looking down through the falling snow he was thinking about his years spent in London. A little out of character, he played memories back to himself, the way he'd seen people do it in films. He remembered coming to the city as an undergraduate, the first day he set foot on campus at King's College, the smell of exhaust and autumn leaves on Aldwych. The taste of the soft tuna and cheese baps that immigrant family sold, wrapped in thin baking paper, from that hole in the wall. What had been the name of that place again? He couldn't remember. He thought about the nurse from Sri Lanka he dated for a few weeks, how he stopped calling her, how she showed up at his dorm, banging on his door. How he didn't open, didn't answer. He remembered his first meeting with Margaret Thatcher, how she'd announced she would come around for supper only a few hours before showing up. She was the Prime Minister then, in her last year. How he didn't remember anything else from that evening. He thought about his first flat in De Beauvoir town, how he walked along Essex Road to Upper Street on Saturdays and usually bought a book of philosophy and ate a hamburger with cheese and bacon, with French fries and a milk shake. How he'd read Nietzsche there in that café on the corner of Islington Green and Upper Street: *Beyond Good and Evil*. He remembered the excitement of reading that book, like a kneading of his bowels, like the night before going on holiday as a boy, the truth of it, the sense of reading something that actually enlightened him. He remembered the wooden tables in that café, the mustard in little squeezing-bottles, labelled *French*? Was that the mustard brand name?

The time since then had sped by on steroids. Where was the waitress who recognised him every weekend? What had happened to all his political opponents? The ones who just didn't want it enough? Because he was sure that was the key to success. To want it harder than anyone else. To never give up.

He remembered the kind of butter they sold at the shop on the corner of Downham Road and Sherborne Street, the feeble packaging it came in, the almost brand-free coffee he bought there as well, the giant loafs of white bread that came in clear plastic wrapping and tasted of nothing and were like airy rocks the next day.

He couldn't help being fascinated by his life so far, the sonic-boom cone-shape it had taken on, how quickly the dull breadth and leisure of his youth had turned into the narrow and exciting fast lane of his late twenties, his thirties and forties. Blinkered was a term people used. But he didn't feel that covered it at all. No, to him it had felt like his duty, to follow his instincts, to get somewhere fast. He felt he'd seen and done plenty. No – he hadn't been blinkered at all – he'd been selective, careful, picky, determined, goal-oriented.

He looked at the falling snow from behind the window. From the ground he was as good as invisible.

What was he supposed to do now?

Someone would be calling. Someone responsible for a group of drivers looking for keys. Someone already dressed for snow-removal. Hatted, gloved and booted. Someone who at first would look to him for advice, for help, until he or she maybe started to suspect. He realised this was most likely it for him. Professionally. The end of the party, the fast lane closing down. He knew he'd gambled. This snow hadn't been part of the plan. This freaky weather. This was what losing felt like? Something unforeseen making itself apparent? He snapped his fingers. Fucking reality intruding. He felt a blow of panic, an instant burst of heat. Then he felt he was going numb, the point of his gaze receding into the back of his head. As if he was suddenly looking at a miniature version of the world, one that kept getting smaller. He felt his muscles slackening. Darker patches appeared either side of his head. Or was this the inside of his skull? On the walls of his brain then, if that was what it was, tiny electric loads discharging, almost pleasantly, against the darkness. The workings of his mind? Shutting down? Dispatching a few last commands? He felt reluctant to give in to these signs. To the darkness growing darker at the edges of his vision. He felt himself drifting off. Going limp. He started shuffling aimlessly around his office, dragging his feet across the thick carpet. What would happen now? Prison? Would someone attempt to shoot him? Stab him? Place a bomb in his mailbox? He dropped onto the leather couch, lay down on his side and closed his eyes. He felt he saw the snowflakes whirling inside his head, faster and faster. He felt he was growing nauseous.

Unless? His whole body reenergised and he sprung to his feet. What was it Bjørn had told him once? Something about his mother? A major snow-removal operation in Norway? Yes. It came back to him now. This thing was apparently legendary. This woman.

/>

/mother_and_son

Started at Thu Sep 14 02:43:37 27020

Command line was: ./henkick_1260 --out-dir=store/
final_rebuild --out-postfix=arx_run_0_no_clean
--creat-sigma=10 --no-plot --save-plot --kwg-
base=hk_kwg_9.db --drives-list=drives.txt --drive-
idx=99

Version tag 3.12.1.1260, built Thu Sep 14 02:43:34
27020

Job ID is: 659124, 1289 instances allocated

VC hash: 8a5db9cf59eb

parsing recovered files at /store/recovery/drvJ6P

<saving_the_world

It had been snowing for nearly five weeks solid, across the whole of Europe. Bjørn's mother Liv woke in her house in Trondheim, Norway, and started packing a large rucksack. Mittens, scarves, wool-underwear, wool-sweaters, super-underwear (synthetic), wool-socks (famous skier brand), some simple jewellery, sweatpants, an extra pair of all-weather trousers and a jacket, a wool headband to warm the ears but not ruin the hair, toiletries in one of those soft see-through plastic beauty bags, five books (of which three were crime-fiction by Jo Nesbø, another was *Hunger* by Knut Hamsun, and the last a biography of Ibsen).

Her husband Odin lay in bed and watched her pack with his head propped on his large hands. It was dark still. He'd made coffee and fetched some chocolate. She felt depressed by the thought of leaving him, felt depressed by the thought of travelling, felt depressed by getting up so early, felt worried in an unspecified way, felt angry with her son Bjørn, felt angry at herself for being angry with Bjørn, felt this was none of her business, felt a little flattered.

How she would love to curl up in her husband's arms. How she hated going out when it was still dark, and windy, and snowing, or raining. How she'd always hated this aspect of autumn and winter. Waking up when it was dark, getting up in the dark, working in the dark, coming home in the dark. The long dark shivering winter. The lurking dread in the early hours of morning, when no one should be out. The lingering sleepiness in the limbs, in the head, behind the eyes, the often sore throat. Her system said no. Her sense of duty dragged her feet forward, lifted her arms, pulled her warm sweater on. She hated it. This was the only thing she knew she really hated. Her arms hurt like hell. Her mood was darkened by this never-ending pain. How about feeling pain-free for once? How about not being in this straightjacket of murmuring dull pain for just one single morning? What was it Bjørn had said? Treatment in the US if all went well? What did he expect? She loved her son, more than anything in the world, but he had a selfish streak. It had always made her cringe. She bet he hadn't even considered a negative response. She'd spoiled him that way.

Odin got up and put his bathrobe back on. They both went downstairs to the kitchen. She turned on the radio. He took out some bread and cheese and ham and other breakfast foods. She said she couldn't eat. He made himself a slice of bread with ham and cheese and mayonnaise. She was saving the world that day? Better have some toast then. She forced it down with brown cheese topped with strawberry jam. He went up and put on clothes. His hair was uncombed and remained so. Brushed his teeth. She cleared the table, put the plates and utensils in the dishwasher. Turned it on, said don't forget to empty this.

In the car they were quiet. The radio played Cher: *If I Could Turn Back Time*. The windscreen wipers made a mechanic squeak for each wipe of the wet snow. The seats started to warm. Crossing over the hill and down to the harbour they could see the ship and its lights. A mist of smoke and vapour was forming around it. She sighed. The snow-removal machines looked like giant drugged insects, all yellow and lit up, chained to the deck (*sleep then, until we wake you and start you and you obey us, she thought*). Odin stopped the car at the bottom of the gangplank. She didn't want to get out. The car was so cosy, so comfortable. Odin smelled so nice. To go back to sleep was what she wanted most of all.

"Take me home again."

He smiled and she knew he wouldn't do it, that she couldn't turn around now. She leant over and kissed him.

"I love you."

"I love you too."

She opened the car door and fetched her rucksack from the boot. As she walked up the gangplank and turned to look at Odin (seated in the car looking at her with his sad moist and friendly eyes), a slice of light blue sky was just about visible to the East, through the falling snow.

/>

<the_power_of_love

At dawn the giant ship slid into coastal waters just off Norfolk. Bjørn's mother was pacing the deck, well clothed, but still feeling the dull chill in her bones from being up so early. She walked in between the yellow-coloured tractors, the towering snow ploughs, the snow-throwers, the mining-style dumpers, the simply unbelievably large H-series *Cab*-snow-removal-machines; her sleeping insect friends, tied down with miles of chain. You could live your whole life in one of these.

It was very quiet. No gulls in the air, no whistling wind. The snow was falling at a slight angle. It seemed light, but was heavy, thick, full of water. The temperature just below 0°C. Atmospheric pressure dropping low. The worst mix of conditions. Snow piling up with serious density. Wind most likely picking up sooner. Not later.

She climbed the gritted staircase up to the ship's bridge with difficulty, as her painful arms refused to bend much above the level of her breasts. She stopped outside the metal-door and leant forward on the railing, catching her breath. From this, the best vantage point on the ship, she saw nothing up ahead, only the snow falling at an angle through the light-cones on the deck below.

"What do you think?"

It was the captain, coming up behind her.

"Oh, I didn't hear you."

"No wonder with all this snow."

"I prefer to wait and see. It's hard to say."

"Yes, you're right."

"Though..."

The captain looked at her.

"No... it's too early to say."

"You've never seen it like this?"

"No, I haven't. And you...?"

The captain looked forward again while she looked at him. His face was red, swollen, his eyes mild and watery, though there was definitely a sense that he knew what he was doing, something about the calmness in his voice, his considerable physique, the captain's hat, the black uniform, the way he just stood there beside her, solidly.

"Well. It's hard to say. Though…" He trailed off, looking hard into the snow.

"…?"

"Once, maybe twice, up around Novaya Zemlya, but, never…"

"Down here?"

"No, yeah, never down here."

"I see."

They both looked ahead as the ship kept making its way forward, seemingly endlessly caught in the same spot.

"Liv… Olsen? Was it?"

"Yes."

"So it was you who managed that situation back in, was it 1987? All that terrible snow in Oslo?"

"Yes."

"And that's why?"

"I think so, it's been a while, but…"

"Sure, but still, you got the call."

"Yes, I did. We'll see."

"Yes, I guess we will. Good luck with it though. We'll be docking at Harwich in an hour."

"Thanks."

She made her way down to her cabin and packed her rucksack, making sure the books and the manual were readily available at the top. Then she sat down on her bunk, closed her eyes and imagined she was on an island in the Aegean, the sand warming her back, her neck, the sweet dry wind of that region, the Meltemi, blowing over her arms and legs, some Jennifer Rush on her Walkman: *The Power of Love.*

/>

<the_harwich_landing

Harwich International port, a dope fiend's shabby paradise on any normal morning, no one about, all windows shut and curtains drawn, the off-licences stocked with cheap high-energy calorific ready-made foodstuffs, a general feeling of gloom and decay and the smell of oil and a tidal basin full of slimy goo. And that morning this pinkie of a town almost invisible from even up close. In just five weeks its houses and roads and gardens and general unpleasantness had all but disappeared under the snow, dope drying up fast, dope takers ensconced, snowed in, shaking, wrapped in blankets.

On the snow-clad quay, looking up at the ship, stood the Mayor of London, his secretary Kirsty, Bjørn and the Norwegian Ambassador. The gangplank was lowered from above. Two gulls squawked as they settled on a large rusty freestanding truss behind the onlookers; then they squawked some more as they took off, shitting invisibly in amongst the snowflakes. Bjørn thought he hadn't heard the sound of sea birds in a long while. Then he saw his mother at the railing, and he waved at her, but she didn't see him.

"Mamma!"

He waved once more, but still she was too focused to notice, trying to make it down the gangplank in one piece.

"Bjørn, is that her?" The Mayor asked.

"Yes, that's her."

"So, what's she like your mother?"

"What do you mean?"

"You know, she's got a reputation, right? Ambassador?"

The Ambassador wore a traditional Norwegian costume, topped with a kind of tramp's hat catching snow all around the rim.

"I don't know her, but yes, she's... I've heard. She can be quite tough."

The traditional costume was cut from cloth that snow liked to hang on to. The Ambassador smiled his endless smile, looking in no direction and at nothing in particular.

"I can't believe... How can you talk like that? Bjørn is right here."

Kirsty shook her head, looked at Bjørn and touched his right arm.

Bjørn found the Ambassador nauseatingly unpleasant to be around. Why he didn't exactly know. It felt like standing next to a Perspex container full of wriggling snakes and slowly climbing spiders. He wished he could have been alone right now – to greet his mother the way he wanted to.

"Mamma!"

She looked up and saw him.

"Bjørn!"

He ran over to the gangplank, to at least be the first to talk to her, to let her know that if he'd really known, if he'd really, really known, he would never have gone, never on that trip to Greenland, he would swear on it, he would've never taken that job with the Mayor, and he would never have dragged her into it, never, if he didn't feel he'd had to.

"My son," she smiled and put down her rucksack.

"Hey Mamma!"

He reached his arms out and they hugged. Her perfume, still Charlie by Revlon, her body, still his mother's, the way he instinctively knew it, even through layers of high-tech sports gear, even though she'd put on twenty kilos since he last saw her.

"Oh," she said, "oh, it's been too long."

"Yes, it has, and, how do you feel?"

"Ah..."

"Your arms I mean? Are you tired?"

"Ah. No. It's nothing I can't, don't think about it. And no... I love being on boats."

She held him at arm's length and looked at him, eyes gleaming.

"My son..."

She hugged him again and Bjørn felt the depths of guilt deepen inside him, though he also felt better.

"I'm sorry."

"Don't talk silly."

"But..."

"I know. I'm your mother."

"I hope you..."

"I do."

They hugged again, and the mix of emotions was too much for Bjørn. He felt his throat tighten, the pressure building behind his eyes. He pulled in some of the instantly flowing mucus, and hearing this she hugged him even tighter. Tears started falling down his cheeks, down her GORE-TEX-covered back. And all the while the snow was covering them, like inert objects, piling up on their shoulders, on their headgear, on her rucksack, on the ground.

/>

<towards_london

Onboard the tracked 56-seater snow coach, making its slow way from Harwich to London: five Foreign and Commonwealth Office senior-rank officials, ten Armed Forces personnel of varying but mostly high rank, including three Generals (Army, Air-force, Navy), the Norwegian Ambassador and his secretary, the Mayor of London and his secretary Kirsty, Bjørn's mother Liv, Bjørn of course, and about fifteen various ranking officials from various offices and various bureaucratic functions.

It was 3 p.m. Bjørn and his mother were sipping aquavit from a hipflask. The relatively new snow coach brought down from Spitsbergen had had to stop five times for basic track maintenance between Harwich and Colchester and then another three times between Colchester and

Brentwood. Something about the watery snow it couldn't handle. Driving mostly along the hard shoulder of the A12, the coach had continually been passing abandoned cars, the coach's passengers whisking away condensation from inside the windows to be able to see out.

As the coach was pulled over for stretching and peeing, on Bjørn's mother's request, at the edge of the London basin, up around Romford, the snow suddenly stopped falling, and for the first time in five weeks, and for no more than four minutes, visibility was restored to something like pre-Neolithic clarity. In the high-contrast light, from the tracked coach's current elevation, Canary Wharf felt like it could be plucked out of the ground, the Gherkin looked edible, the London Eye looked like a circus hoop for poodles, so white, so unreal, so small, the Shard, well, like a bad imitation of a shard. A crack in the cover of cloud had opened like a vulva in early labour, and a shaft of light was coming down, dramatically holding everything still. It was like the scene pulsated, breathed heavy, its time arrested. The clarity of it made Bjørn afraid. From out of nowhere he started thinking about bathroom fixtures and door-hinges and types of glass and window-frames and shop-signs and asphalt edges and road-lights and screw type vs. bayonet bulbs, the type of brick used, the quality of cement, the welding points between two steel columns in a skyscraper. He felt that these things held a message.

He shuddered and zipped up his trousers. His feet were getting wet. Then the crack closed, swiftly, and the light was sucked back up to the heavens. As they climbed onboard the snow coach it started snowing again, even denser and wetter than before, and Bjørn took his seat next to his mother.

/>

What kind of snow were you dealing with? For how long had it been snowing as you reached your area of operation? Temperature fluctuations? Had there been time for ice to form underneath? Note that this could, in worst-case scenarios, only take a minimum of 24 hours with a thaw and a subsequent freeze. What did the terrain look like? Were there slopes? What percentage of your area of operation was of a 10% incline or more? Note that this could impact fuel-calculations, chain-tearage rates, staff-exhaustion coefficients, precision-of-depth-of-plough vs.

type-of road-surface calculations, clutch and break-pad costs. Were there speed bumps? If yes, how did you plan to handle the issue? Did your budget allow for *shaving* of said speed bumps? Were you operating in an area where the location of said speed bumps were indicated above 100 cm of the road-surface? If not, how did you plan to tackle the issue?

Let's say it had been snowing for five weeks solid without any form of removal intervention, what would be your first priority? Your ten immediate actions?

How did you get your machinery in place? How did you make sure your machinery stayed functional? Say no roads were clear from your point zero of clearing, from where you were, so to speak, on level ground, 300+ of the largest and most cumbersome but also most powerful snow-removal machines in the world at your disposal, where did you park and maintain those machines that couldn't be employed? Fuelling facilities? Related fire-hazards? Remember, snow also burned when soaked with fuel. Pavements? What kind? Road surface? Asphalt? Cobblestone? Concrete? Road shoulders? What kind? Soft? Hard? Medium? Did you speak the local language? If not, you should make sure to bring your diagram ring binder. Remember though that certain diagrams/symbols might appear funny/offensive in different territories.

Absolutely not to forget: where were you planning to dispose of all the snow?

How did you make an adequate reconnaissance of possible dumping-spots? Remember the consequences of dumping too many loads too rapidly in an inadequate location. Think water vs. slope, visibility, Archimedes' law, traction, wind-direction, population density, access. Staff? Were you going to recruit locally? If so, what qualifications would constitute your baseline? How did you make sure someone was telling you the truth about his or her ability? Did you need to establish a test and training facility? Were you planning to do so-called *flat recruiting*? Or, would you be skill-set sensitive? Let's say horse and carriage experience far outweighed tractor and dumpster skills in your area of operation. Did you go down a composite route or bring up the mediaeval rear as soon as possible? Advantages and disadvantages of over-focusing temporary training programs on backing-up skills for vehicles five tons plus? Should you consider a blanket ban on all backing up if your average available skill-set was pre-motorised? Could you monetarily justify ploughing in straight lines and circles? Did the area's topography allow such actions? Etc.

/>

<drinking_talking

Bjørn, Wolfgang and the Dane's apartment, Shadwell,
London. Wolfgang hadn't been home for the last five weeks.
No one knew where he was. The Dane was in his room,
feeling depressed, looking for season five of the TV/DVD
series The West Wing somewhere under all the mess,
hoping to have found it before the one hour electricity slot
at 10 p.m. (in five minutes). His girlfriend Alice was asleep
on the smelly futon in the corner, all dressed.

Bjørn and his mother sat in the living room, an almost
empty bottle of Linie Aquavit on the table between them.
They'd come down from Harwich that day, in the snow
coach. Bjørn's mother had refused hotel accommodation
together with the official snow-removal delegation, knowing
that hotels were most likely the first places to be looted

and burned after shops and restaurants. Outside, it was still snowing. They'd tried to open the balcony doors, but with no luck; thick ice had already formed at the bottom of the one and a half metre layer of snow.

Bjørn's mother looked around the sublimely cluttered room, at all the stuff the three men had accumulated but not been able to sort or store in any form of order – all kinds of cables for numerous electrical devices rolled up or pushed behind something larger, colourful document folders on every conceivable surface, the data-side of innumerable DVDs gleaming in at least twelve places, paper-plates softening quietly, used plastic cutlery losing elasticity, fast-food packaging going pale, newspapers yellowing, several old mobile phones, loose sheets of paper seemingly floating in the air, about six cacti unwatered for months, smudged napkins, all kinds of bolts and screws, power-tools, spare cycling equipment, old toothbrushes, dried-out pens, broken pencils, numerous IKEA instruction manuals (and left-over parts), manuals for all kinds of electronic devices, several bongo drums gathering dust, an old beat-up guitar without strings. You name it.

"It's not so bad here," she said, to be polite.

"It's terrible. I'm sorry."

"Where's Kirsty staying?"

"I don't know, with the Mayor I guess."

"You like her?"

"Is it that obvious?"

"I'm your mother, remember."

"Want some peanuts?"

"No. Gives me an itchy throat."

"By the way, how are your arms?"

"Not so bad with this inside…"

She picked up the bottle of aquavit and poured them both another drink, emptying the bottle. Bjørn's head dropped down to his chest but jerked right back up again.

"Good. You'll…"

"Skål!"

They both knocked back their shot.

"… you'll sleep in my room."

"And you?"

"Here, on the beanbag. It's big enough."

"God. That's true. Enormous. Who bought that?"

"Wolfgang I think."

"Do you have any more of this?"

She pointed to the empty bottle. Bjørn nodded and got up slowly, stepped over five whatever the hell they were on the floor, and got down on his knees in the corner of the kitchen by the washing machine, among the billiard-ball-sized spheres of lint – removed the bottom cover and fished out a bottle of Glenfiddich.

"Ice?"

"He he... yeah."

"He he."

They laughed quietly for a while. Then they dried their eyes while Bjørn got some ice-cubes from the freezer (unbelievably still working with only a few hours of electricity per day). He poured them a drink. They stared out through the large floor-to-ceiling balcony windows for a while, hypnotised by the snow's continued falling motion; from being drunk.

/>

After saying goodnight to his mother and passing out on the beanbag, as the snow kept falling over London, there was an image in Bjørn's mind. The image was of the person Bjørn considered to be himself. This person was wearing a purple coloured tuxedo with yellow coloured socks. The tuxedo trousers were hanging halfway down the owner's legs exposing a pair of crumbled shirttails and a flaccid penis sticking out sort of like a rodent from its den. That was the image the mind saw, partly by looking down itself and partly as an image taken from a few metres away, creating a composite picture of being present in, and at the same time, distant from itself.

The main emotion conjured by this image was shame. The second emotion was bewilderment. The next image in the sequence of images no one would remember was of the purple-clad mind walking up a steep road in drifting snow, thinking to itself that it had better get home and get changed. The mind was walking up a road it remembered from experience. It knew that this road was leading home. The owner of this dream knew he needed to get home and get changed. His trousers were still halfway down his thighs. His socks were too colourful to go with the purple tuxedo. The feeling in the dream was a very strong longing for this place that felt like home, at the end of the steep road, through the snowfall.

No one would remember this dream. As far as the physical world was concerned, this sequence of emotions and images had not existed. The mind experienced it-self walking poorly dressed in a space it registered as disappearing into obscurity in a vague distance from what felt like the centre of the space itself. Behind and to the left and to the right the snowdrift tapered off into a black nothingness. There was a sense of great urgency.

And then a realisation took place. It felt like the plane of reality segmented into four superimposed layers of parallel truth, of which there was in each layer a place called home, but in different places. Bjørn's mind realised that the place it wanted to go to used to be home, once. The powerful longing home was replaced by a hollow disappointment. The mind knew it would only get to a house where his family lived no more. The mind had stacked five or six different geographies that now, when the layers had stratified, were obviously different routes home to different places Bjørn had been able to call home in the last twenty years. In his drunken dream he realised that the place he thought he was going to was now surely occupied by someone else.

The drunken dream's mind took out a mobile phone from a tuxedo pocket and held it up to its ear. The mind felt like calling Bjørn's mother, to tell her he was on his way home, to their old house – that someone else was living there now. But what it heard as it held the phone up to its ear was his mother talking to another person, and no matter how much he wanted to say something to get her attention he couldn't. He was listening to a separate conversation she was having with a stranger.

/>

<breakfast_for_two

Bjørn woke on the beanbag with the smell and feeling of synthetic dust in his nostrils. He'd been aware of his hangover in his sleep, blurrily assessing its size and genus, whether it would include stomach-issues. If he held his breath the thumping in his head stopped for a second, but then it returned with a bass drum as he inhaled and exhaled again. He tried to massage his temples, to put some pressure on the sinuses, to no avail. He needed to pee. He wasn't sure he'd make it to the toilet without throwing up on the way. The light shining through the uncurtained floor-to-ceiling windows felt clean. Strong. Was his mother up yet?

He rolled off the beanbag and pushed himself onto his knees, assessing the potential impact of getting all the way upright, and then to the bathroom. It felt risky. His mouth watered already. In a semi-stoop he ran to the kitchen nook and puked into the sink, turning on the tap, seeing the water rise, the rest of yesterday's meagre dinner coming up the sides with it, a few peanuts, something that looked like beans (though he hadn't had beans). He tried to pump the plug a few times with his hand reluctantly extended into the stew. A few bubbles rose but nothing moved. He was only wearing his boxers and was shivering. He shouted as the pain of the cold water contracted the muscles in his hand. The acid smell of his puke made him gag once more. He bent over, turned on the tap (a reflex) and let the yellow bile drop from his mouth into the already immobile red.

He found some old newspaper in the corner and started soaking and lifting and disposing the stinking liquid into a triple-lined plastic bag. He worked determined, though he needed to pee badly. He thought he heard someone go to the bathroom. He tied the plastic bags five times over and left the budle by the full and overflowing trashcan. The sink was draining slowly again when he tried to wash away the residues. He dried his face and blew his nose in a tea-towel. Someone flushed the toilet. Then there was an insistent silence, as if the lack of outside noise from the street, or the radio, or TV, or footsteps or human voices, had tuned the air into white noise, a standing wave that would've escaped if he'd been able to open the window.

He walked over to the beanbag and put on yesterday's clothes, the underwear neatly embedded in the thermal pants, feeling himself shivering from somewhere deep within, his head ballooning and contracting with each heartbeat, the taste in his mouth a rancid cod-liver oil, an old plate of hair-sprouting lasagne, the afterglow of kebab meat, foods he hadn't had for ages. The door from the hallway opened and he turned and saw his mother enter, thermal underwear on, her downy short hair uncoiffed, her eyes red. She resembled a fertility goddess from Asia Minor, the way she'd expanded between her head and knees.

"Up already?"

"Not sure," he replied and hurried past her to the toilet, to pee, to brush his teeth and look for a painkiller.

Coming back he saw her sitting by the table, glass of water in hand, staring out the large floor-to-ceiling windows, not really looking at the snow, but somehow through it, beyond it, lost in thought. Her face had changed so much since he saw it last. It was painful to realise. At the same time it was comforting to have her near. The weight she'd put on had sanded out the wrinkles on her throat and forehead. The fuller cheeks had concentrated the aging process around her nose and eyes, like rivulets run dry between smooth and higher sandbanks. There was a yellow hue next to the red going all the way round her eyes, fishlike, gelatinous. This was painful to observe. She looked tired, but not just from last night. It was tiredness accumulated. Too much wine, too much to think about, too many nights reading, too little time to get all she needed to do done, a ponderous character like hers, someone who didn't take important things lightly, at least when she thought she could have an impact. Tossing and turning until the beeping of the alarm.

How many years since they'd last met? Three? Four? It could be as many as five. Though they'd spoken on the phone now and then.

He fetched himself some water and lit the primus for some instant coffee. He searched the cupboards for biscuits but found none. What were they supposed to eat? Not that he could hold anything down. But in all the stress of organising his mother's arrival he'd forgotten to stock up on essentials. These days you couldn't just nip out for some bread and eggs. It required planning. He found some prawn-cocktail crisps behind the Dane's recently purchased family-sized tub of Ovaltine. It would have to do.

What else had changed about her? She seemed shorter, though that could be an effect of growing wider. He hadn't noticed up in Harwich, or on the coach, or last night, but she was quieter too, or more distant. She looked sad, sitting there, eyes red, yellow and watery, focused on nothing, like her soul had flown out for a moment and she already missed it.

Maybe she was assessing the situation, now that they'd met, had become drunk and had woken up again. Maybe it was sinking in, finally, in this decrepit apartment, among the balls of dust on the floor – the impossibility of it?

"How are you this morning?"

She turned and smiled, absentmindedly.

"How was my bed? Not too hard I hope?"

"No, it was fine. Thanks for making your room so tidy."

"Ah, that was nothing."

"Still. It's nice when..."

She looked out the large windows again, into the static falling snow. She seemed to be in pain. She held her shoulders high.

"It's nice when someone... makes an effort."

She looked around the clutter of the room, the total absence of planning in the way things were laid out or just left behind, mostly on the floor. Bjørn remembered the lack of breakfast food and felt an urge to puke again. He felt restless and worried in an unspecified way, as if he'd forgotten to do something important, something essential. The water was boiling on the primus and he got up to make them coffee.

As he poured the hot water over the granules he couldn't stop thinking how awkward it was to see his mother in this context, in this shit-hole apartment, where nothing was the way he wanted it to be. She sat there worried, overweight, older – looking into the snow, the infinite stuff it was her task to deal with. A person like any other. And of course, at the same time, not like anyone else at all. This was the only other person for him, really. Everyone else were just shadows of her, contrast-losers, even when she'd changed the way she had, gotten so much closer to death, so fast. The potato-glow of her skin spoke directly to him, the widening pores across her nose had something to say, the thin lines of red in her cheeks, like feather paint, what looked like the beginnings of a hump on her back, the wrinkles around her knuckles. She seemed statuesque, at the same time completely vulnerable.

He gave her a cup of coffee and sat down opposite, both staring out the large windows. The snow was being whipped into mini-twisters here and there, as if someone was playing with it, stirring the atmosphere with an invisible cocktail stick. The falling snowflakes joined indifferently, became small parts of the localised rotating funnels.

Looking at it Bjørn felt instant panic. He started grinding his teeth, clutching and shaking the warm mug, hot coffee spilling over his fingers.

"Bjørn!"

He looked at his mother.

"What is it Bjørn?"

He put the mug down on the wobbly table and felt the burning pain in his hands.

"What's the matter?"

His mother looked spooked. She tried to lean across the table to comfort him, but couldn't reach, which made her look even more helpless, more lost.

He tried to smile. He couldn't tell her what it was. It was too ephemeral. Unexplainable really, to another person.

He looked at his mother. He hadn't seen her in five years. He tried to remember what she'd looked like as a younger woman. He recalled a few photos from an old album. A powerful smile she'd had. This person was still there, but padded out, wearier, calcifying. Her movements weren't spontaneous anymore, but had to be planned to avoid as much pain as possible.

"You look just like your father, do you know that? You remind me so much of him, when he was your age."

Bjørn felt calmer.

"Yeah?"

He didn't like being compared to his father.

"Yes, he'd sometimes do what you just did. Some kind of thing would come over him and he wouldn't be able to tell me about it. Shouting sometimes. It was always terrifying. I could see he was in pain, something he was thinking about wouldn't let him alone. It made us more distant I think, that I couldn't comfort him. Though I tried."

"I'm sorry," Bjørn said.

"No you don't have to be. *I'm* sorry. I just thought you'd like to know. But it's probably not helpful. I know."

He felt like hugging her.

"No. It is. I didn't know that about him."

"There's perhaps a lot you don't know about him, or me. Or our life together, before the divorce. But maybe we'll find time to talk about it now that I'm here?"

Bjørn didn't know if he actually wanted to know.

"I think it would be good for you. And me too perhaps. We got a start last night, didn't we?"

"Did we? I really don't remember. What did we talk about?"

"Oh."

She looked out the window at the snow. He felt he was disappointing her.

"Nothing important. I'll tell you again some other time. Headache?"

'Terrible."

"Me too. Stomach?"

"Not good."

"Same here. OK, let me see what I can find. I bought some pills in Sweden a few months ago. I think I brought some with me. It's that or some... What do they call it? Hair off the ducks?"

Bjørn swallowed a considerable amount of matter from a treacherous burp.

As she got up to leave she leant over the back of his chair and gave him a long hug.

/>

<cool_down

In London things cooled down. Fast. Under the snow. Trees cooled down. Buildings cooled down. The ground cooled down. Plastic became brittle. Toenails bit their owners, at least that's what it felt like. Shins blasted by cold wind through a thin trouser felt like they were catching fire inside, paradoxically. It was quite well known in colder parts of the world that when people froze to death they undressed as the last thing they did, feeling so warm all of a sudden, unbearably warm. Bitter cold was known to feel like fire in the bones. Polar explorers had been found many years later, a solid statue in the snow, on their knees, naked, their arms outstretched, a serene smile on their face, eyes still open. Cold through and through. As cold as the surrounding air, that body which was once thirty-seven degrees constantly.

Asphalt got cold. Snow under layers of more snow on top of cold asphalt became ice, thick, solid, nearly see-through left long enough. Bronze statues, no point even mentioning how cold they got. Shoes got cold. Shop-windows got cold, ice-crystals formed in the corners, first; then the whole window became a two-sided sheet of ice. Paper carton cooled down as fast as thin metal, almost. Eggs froze and cracked. The sewage got colder, ran slower. Lukewarm water no longer ran in pipes under ground once the boilers started shutting down. Wax got cold. Butter froze. Things that were once warm got cold. The warm city with its men and women sweating in bars, on busses, down in the tube, cycling to work, it cooled down.

The pace of things slowed, as the snowflakes kept swirling faster. All kinds of locks and doors became unbelievably difficult to open with the drifting snow on the ground blowing across bare fingers that fiddled with a small key or a 4-digit code. Over just a few weeks, it got so much colder. Then, over the next months it all froze up. The metropolis' metabolism shut down, dropped to survival mode, like a body would cut off circulation to its extremities in a state of shock.

There was something peaceful about it. Something aesthetically pleasing. Something graceful when something so large cooled down. A sigh of relief. A culling of minor thoughts. Some major ones too. A clearer air. Quieter. After so much heat for so long. After so much expelled energy.

/>

/others

Started at Fri Sep 15 03:24:15 27020

Command line was: ./henkick_1261 --out-dir=store/final_rebuild --out-postfix=arx_run_0_no_clean --creat-sigma=10 --no-plot --save-plot --kwg-base=hk_kwg_9.db --drives-list=drives.txt --drive-idx=100

Version tag 3.12.1.1261, built Fri Sep 15 03:24:12 27020

Job ID is: 835279, 1103 instances allocated

VC hash: 5d4ca7fe23db

parsing recovered files at /store/recovery/drvG1H

<the_centre_for_climate_

studies_staff_reading_room

Wolfgang sat on an uncomfortable sofa in the staff reading room of the newly established Centre for Climate Studies, a room perched at the top of the Library of the London School of Economics and Political Science. He was looking out at the first snowflakes falling so peacefully from above, settling on the rooftops all around him. From his position he could only partly make out St. Paul's Cathedral, as it was rapidly getting shrouded in a snowy fog. A few pulsating lights were showing on top of the skyscrapers in the City.

His plan had been to cycle home and shut himself in his room to sleep, and then to wake up early Saturday and rehearse for his band's show that same evening. But now he was stuck, or at least, *cycling home* had been dealt a major meteorological blow. Wolfgang hadn't been on a bus in two years and hardly ever took the tube. He'd almost forgotten how to get home by public transport.

He sat with one foot pulled up under his right thigh, his left arm across the back of the uncomfortable sofa. The magazines on the coffee table in front of him were devoted to economic analysis, political commentary, geo-political security, ecological sustainability, trade agreements, third-world development, scientific discovery in the areas of fuel efficiency and carbon capture and storage. The room was intended as a space where researchers could relax and unwind and chat about their lives and whatever else should come to mind between reading reports on famine-induced deforestation in equatorial Africa and writing a paper on the effects of the rekindled ethnic wars of the former USSR.

It was a room created in the spirit of community. Its favourable placement in the Centre's limited geography was testimony to the ambition bestowed upon it by the Centre's leaders, so also its panoramic view of the City of London (had it not been snowing), its rather spacious flooring with nothing placed on it, its walls covered with, if not original art, at least high-quality reproductions of European Modernist classics, well framed and suitably spaced and lit.

Wolfgang had worked at the Centre for nearly a year and

this was the first time he was in there. He was alone, he thought, not having heard anyone cough or close a door or whisper or anything else since Shilpa, his research assistant, had left at 7.30 p.m. A humming from the climate-control system above him and a low fizzing sound of heated water running in pipes behind him were quite audible.

Wolfgang considered the subdued lighting, the new modern-looking shelving system, the scattered serious magazines, the well-framed art, the generous-sized pillows, the thick cream-coloured carpet with another even thicker carpet on top of it, the relatively hard but stylish sofa he sat on. He thought about the load of work sitting on his desk. He watched the snow outside, still falling slowly and somehow eternally.

He kept sitting there, one foot under his thigh, caught in the mid-distance between two other bodies of superior mass, each pulling at him with equal strength, the beauty of the falling snow on the one side and the unknowable reach of his yet unfinished work on the other. What made him move in the end was a sudden and desperate need to piss. His mind gathered in an instant and he got up and felt terribly cold and walked fast towards the men's, cartoonishly shaking and rubbing his hands, determined to face the snow once his bladder was empty.

/>

<the_awareness_took_it_all

[memetic error: possible scrambled file]

In the air above London, in amongst the snowflakes, the Awareness felt it was taking it all in. It saw Wolfgang leave the London School of Economics around 10 p.m. It shook its head benignly as he got on his bike. It knew Kweku was working the night shift over at St. Paul's Cathedral. It had a sense of an upcoming meeting between the two. It could be everywhere all at once, it felt like. It registered the increasing depth of snow on the ground in Regent's Park. It tallied the number of car-crashes on the Inner Ring. It computed the growing slipperiness of the road-surface of Highgate Hill. Pigeons and mice and rats and foxes were communicating with it, letting it know what was happening under ground. It saw the stalled tube-train in the tunnel between Chalk Farm and Belsize Park. It appeared to the Awareness that someone was blowing hard down on Piccadilly Circus with a giant leaf-blower, from high above. It saw the masses of individuals spreading home on foot, from the centre of town, as if carried on the current of air from that giant leaf-blower. It intercepted phone-conversations, for a while, the desperation in the voices, the plans made. Early evening it heard a buzzing as of a swarm of bees, knew it was the sound of conversations, of the millions of conversations Londoners were having on their way home, in their homes. The buzzing faded gradually over a few hours – by early morning on the second day it was just a faint, almost imagined tinnitus ringing. It registered the total mobile network signal blackout at around 1 a.m. It kept track of the power-grid, saw it as an EKG, realised it was in bad shape. It sensed the way the dropping temperature was making steel contract, how this was freeing up space in the joints between load-bearing beams in more recent constructions. It heard the breaking of thousands of windowpanes, as a result of both widespread looting and multiple structural weaknesses in the way the glass had been made, as well as fastened. It felt the slowing down of the sewage system. It felt like this was an instinctive storing up of energy, a city-wide cramp, a bowel movement postponed. It perceived the whiteness of rooftops all around. The fading of light from public lamp-posts. It tried to focus on individual snowflakes, to catalogue their variations. It rejoiced in this infinitude of creation. It felt like the complexity in design was both random and planned. The Awareness knew it had to go into the details of the human suffering caused by the snow. *That* was *its* lot here in Life. It was neither depressed nor bothered by this fact. It registered and accepted things. That was its way. It was as if the Awareness was a conductor having a pre-work coffee, planning the recording session ahead, leafing through the score. It was all the while picking up a radio show. People were calling in, giving updates on the traffic situation, on how they were coping. "Got to be strong," a caller said. "I believe we all second that," the host answered. The Awareness also had a finger on most packets of information travelling across the Internet. It was more or less getting the same thing there, as it was through the radio, though quite a bit more desperate in tone, lonely-sounding. By midnight the energy-grid had its first complete collapse, knocking out both the radio and the web (and the TV of course). It knew that planes were crashing all over Europe. It felt that things were changing, that something was up ahead, a major uncertainty. This was nothing new in the Awareness's experience. For a moment it got distracted again by the millions and millions of snowflakes. It felt to the Awareness like it flew around and photographed them. All of them. A few were so large it needed several shots to capture them completely. To really capture their intricacy. Then the Awareness realised that London was actually snowing under, like covering up in snow, and it stopped flitting around looking at individual snowflakes. It saw Wolfgang falling off his bike, close to the stairs of St Paul's chatedral. The lock fastened on his backpack jamming into his ribs, a few bone fragments pushing into his lungs, close to his heart. It saw the night watchman rush over to help him. It felt like it saw everything all at once. Things would change. It knew.

/>

<passing_out

With an arresting pain clutching the left side of his body, Wolfgang was trying to breathe. Hanging with one arm around the night watchman's neck, his feet not really touching the ground, he only managed tiny sips of air, and for every sip it was like someone jabbed a crowbar into his side. It was such an all-consuming pain that he fainted four or five times on the way from where he fell to past the revolving doors into the nave of the cathedral. He remembered seeing the revolving doors through the snow, moving close to them and reading the frosted inscription on one of the glass panes: *This is no other than the house of God / This is the gate of heaven.* He remembered vaguely laughing at this pompousness and at the same time feeling deeply reassured that he was being carried into a church, even if the person carrying him was a total stranger. Though why would a cathedral be fitted with revolving doors?

Then he passed out again.

/>

<kwekus_magnets

Kweku turned Wolfgang over on his back. He remembered a man stung by a bee as he was repairing a roof, back in Ghana, who within five minutes fell like a drunken cow to the ground, never to get up again, buried in the red soil before the week was over. The meeting with the floor had given Wolfgang's right eye a pretty nice shiner. Kweku was carefully slapping his face to wake him up.

Kweku had been in the UK just about 8 months. His fake papers were all in order, though not strictly bona fide, of course. He knew the High Commissioner's driver, and the High Commissioner's driver had a direct channel to the High Commissioner's heart. So in case so-called push had to come to so-called shove, in the last instance, he wouldn't be, he hoped, in too bad a position. He just had to remember that his name was Moses, that his reason for being there was to study business and law at the London Oxford Institute on Hackney Road, which was true, he did.

He was worried about the man passed-out on the floor before him. He didn't think about himself. He felt if things were meant to be they were meant to be and there was precious little he could do to change that. He'd started feeling this way recently. There was a massive magnet out there in the future that dragged us along, up against whose pull there was very little each of us could do. His take on life was that the more you resisted the magnet, the more trouble you'd get in. He felt this to be fairly self-evident. For if you had a huge magnet pulling you along, and this magnet was set on a course you didn't know, then why try to resist it? No. That was stupid. The only way Kweku could see some form of freedom was to somehow get close enough to the magnet to create a bit of slack on the leash, or perhaps even get on a par with it, and thereby act as gracefully and as free as it did.

But thinking about freedom from the magnet was a plain wrong way to think about it anyway. Accept your magnet, he thought. Don't fight it. Grasp your life for what it is and embrace *that life* without too much doubt. And how did you know where the magnet was? It was easy with a bit of practice. Everybody instinctively knew where his or her magnet was. The magnet was where you felt the least pulled apart. It made sense. When you were hugging the magnet you and it were one. The magnet was your spiritual home, where the stars aligned when you were born, the only place that felt like home to your spirit, to your soul. Kweku knew everybody knew where their magnet was if they only took two minutes to think about it. Though the magnet was an unpredictable entity and would quickly turn around and go another way, say as a reaction to some other magnet's path, say a sister magnet or a mother or father magnet, even a stranger's magnet. Kweku didn't think the magnet thought that the magnet belonged anywhere in particular. If all the magnets, say, of all the people of Ghana wanted to stay in Ghana he knew that every Ghanaian would still be in Ghana. This was simple magnet logic.

Once you got the magnet and its ways you didn't worry so much. You just relaxed and enjoyed the ride. There was no point resisting. No point wondering why. Magnets were magnets. They pushed and pulled. We were all at our magnet's mercy. Your magnet, when you thought about it, was you.

So why wasn't this man waking up?

/>

<soup_everlasting

It felt to Wolfgang as though he was falling deeper into a whiteness. Then he recognised himself. He was aged nine, sitting at the kitchen table watching his father and grandfather (through the window) carrying toilet porcelain prototype after prototype from the garden shed into the cellar whose entrance was external and underneath the window where Wolfgang was sitting watching. The night before he'd dreamt that a large multicoloured bird had entered his open bedroom window and laid down on his pillow and there started morphing into different kinds of animal, but remaining the same size. The bird had felt like it was wise. Wolfgang had woken up with a sense of having seen something extraordinary, but hadn't told anyone about the dream. It was approaching lunch-hour. His grandfather and father usually finished their work around 12.30 p.m. on Saturdays, so would be coming into the kitchen soon, all scrubbed up and hungry. Wolfgang's mother stood by the stove whisking cream of potato soup. She was singing hymns. In between her hymns she would ask Wolfgang questions from his catechism. Wolfgang wondered what would happen if the kitchen collapsed and they fell down into the cellar. He imagined it would hurt quite a lot, maybe even kill them, particularly now that they would hit their heads and other body parts against the many toilet porcelain prototypes his father and grandfather had been stacking. He felt the unspoken wisdom of the morphing many-coloured bird from his dream as a warm feeling in his upper body. He heard his father and grandfather emerging from the cellar, the cellar door falling shut and the padlock locking. Then he saw their heads as they straightened their backs and brushed the cellar dust off their clothes. He imagined what would happen if he shot a large blade out of his palm, whether it would bounce around the kitchen in straight angles or get stuck in the wall. He thought his father and grandfather looked small when he looked at them from above. He couldn't hear what they were saying. He saw the smoke from his grandfather's pipe coming up from his turned-away head, as if his head was on fire. He thought it might as well be, seeing how old he was by then, that it wouldn't surprise him if old people spontaneously combusted, or started fuming and glowing like poorly oxygenated fires. He knew that people in Hell were dealing with very high temperatures on a daily basis, so that, if his grandfather was going there, as his mother said he would, then high heat would be something he would have to get used to soon, and maybe he was already half-way there. Wolfgang didn't fear the idea of Hell as much as he thought his mother's stories called for. His grandfather had told him it would be much more fun in Hell than in the other place, and in any case, much more fun than he was having then and there, every day listening to his daughter *speaking in tongues*, as he called it. Wolfgang thought *speaking in tongues* meant talking really fast or with much enthusiasm. He too got tired of his mother's stories about the baby Jesus and all the disciples and the many acts of kindness, although he believed them. "Enough," his grandfather would say. "And you'll be sorry in Hell," his mother would reply, and Wolfgang's grandfather would bite into a sugar-cube, sip some coffee, and with his face half-hidden from Wolfgang's mother, wink and smile at him. The bird in Wolfgang's dream had felt like it could exist both in Heaven and Hell. Heaven to Wolfgang was like a large newly made bed. He wouldn't mind going there. He liked sleeping. He enjoyed dreaming. He seldom had nightmares. His father and grandfather entered the kitchen. He put away his Bible and started laying the table. Both his father and grandfather ruffled his hair, smiled at him and sat down. Wolfgang felt safe. Felt the bird from his dream flying into the heavenly bedroom, then coming out again through one of heaven's many windows and sitting down on a branch just above the garden-shed where the toilet prototypes had been stored until that day. Pouring the soup into a terrine his mother was singing a hymn and, unusually, both his father and grandfather started singing along, looking at each other and smiling, a little secretly, Wolfgang thought, and Wolfgang's father put his arm around his wife's waist as she placed the steaming soup-terrine on the table. Wolfgang felt secure and happy. He enjoyed Saturday afternoons and was looking forward to this one in particular as his grandfather had promised to take him for a drive, and maybe even to see a game of football (but not to tell his mother). They started eating in silence. When his grandfather's spoon dropped into his bowl, sending a spray of warm soup towards the window, Wolfgang thought it was only one of his many jokes and laughed and smiled at him, but his grandfather didn't smile back, and with what Wolfgang later remembered as panicked eyes, his grandfather's head and torso crashed forward across the table, sending the soup-terrine flying.

/>

<kwekus_lessons

Kweku threw Wolfgang onto his left shoulder, fireman-like, and held him there with one arm while with his other he formed a cover for his eyes. What now then magnet, he thought. Where to? He felt strong and steady despite the weight of another man on his shoulder. But where to?

The snow was abominable. Blinding, stinging. He didn't know how slippery the pavement was. But maybe it wasn't slippery if he didn't think it was? He was making good headway, direction east. But why that way? What was out there? That he knew of? That would solve this pickle? Get him out of it? He knew nothing there, but still, he had to choose a direction. He couldn't just stand paralyzed covering up with snow. So east then, it was better than nothing.

He felt with overwhelming certainty that this would be fine. Maybe this was normal for London? Weather like this. He just had to walk him somewhere warm. He was breathing still. He wasn't dead yet. His magnet was probably just tired. It happened to all magnets. It wasn't really a problem. Though it was harsh, this weather, even if it was normal. How did they do it? Londoners? The wind blew straight through his thin trousers. He felt his magnet would be alright. In a situation when things seemed hopeless you just had to listen, that was the way. Just listen. Where the body felt a pull you should go. There was always a pull somewhere. His magnet had a lock on his guts. That was where the invisible harness sat, around the waist, coupled through the navel, some invisible umbilical cord fastened to the elements of chance, always in motion, like everything else, like all things, connected, all lives tied to other lives, invisibly, but tied. Oh yes, tied. Together. You just had to push your ego aside, your vanity, yourself. It would tell you, friend, where to go. You could only go one place at a time. No one could please everyone. No, no one. This was lesson number one. Lesson number two: to wait and see and have no hurry. A solution would always come, a pull, a way to go. You had to be ready then. And not fight yourself. To breathe through the nose, that was lesson number three.

He didn't slip. He didn't fall. He carried Wolfgang along, eastwards, slowly. So far he was just a few hundred metres from the big cathedral doors, from *The Gates of Heaven, The House of God*. With another man on his shoulder.

Lesson number four: to keep looking forward. No matter what. The past was the past. That was where you were. The magnet pulled you away from there. There was no reason to look back. Ahead was the life you would live. Time passed you by, like a herd of buffalo. Steady. In cycles like that. Came around again. Day and night. Night and day. And then one day: you were no longer there when the herd came round. You were gone. They didn't know. They didn't care. But this man on Kweku's shoulders wasn't dead yet. He would see the buffalos again, he felt sure of it. He would see the herd in the dust again.

He pushed on, step by remarkable solid step, past Godliman St. in a frothing whiteness, shimmering with cones of atmospheric streetlight at regular intervals.

Lesson number five: to take a rest before you fell among the apples. You only had so much energy. You spent it all, like an empty bottle of beer, you remained in the street. You saved a little, someone would carry you a little further. Lesson number six: the earth and heaven were your friends. You sometimes thought you were alone. You sometimes felt afraid. Why didn't the stars fall on your head? Why didn't the earth open up a hole for you? No. Heaven and earth were your friends. You walked among the elements. On a crust of the earth. Sometimes there was wind. Sometimes rain. Sometimes snow. You walked upside down, and you didn't fall off! You jumped up and down and you didn't sag into the ground! There was balance. You walked in the middle. You talked and laughed, and one day, of a sudden, your words and sounds were gone. What then? The sky, the heaven, they'd kept you calm. The earth, the ground, it had kept you fed.

Lesson number seven, last lesson: life was like a dream, life was like an afternoon nap. You woke from a nap and felt life in your chest. The magnet woke you up. You knew you'd been gone, you'd dreamt of something you'd never seen before. Life was like that. There was nothing you could do. Nothing. You could breathe through your nose, lesson number three, remember, was the most important lesson.

Past the National Firefighters Memorial in the small park among the taller buildings. He crossed the street there, behind an abandoned bus, and started cutting south towards the river. He moved steady, very steady, down into the pedestrian zone on Peter's Hill.

/>

<night_watchmen

Kweku had stopped and was leaning against and peering into the windows of a large sort of modern redbrick building down by the Thames. The weight of Wolfgang was momentarily shifted from his shoulder to the wall and the window frame. It was getting heavy. It seemed there was a bridge over the river further down, to the left, but he wasn't sure, and it didn't feel right to be crossing a river in any case. Not in this weather.

There was a light on, several lights actually, in this building, and Kweku thought he'd seen a shadow moving in there, so now he was carefully tapping the window to see if he couldn't attract the shadow and maybe get some help. Wolfgang was still out cold and getting colder. He needed help. Fast.

"Hello."

Kweku couldn't locate the source of the voice. He turned three-sixty.

"Here."

The voice sounded familiar.

"Where?"

"This way."

It was as if he'd heard the voice before. The snowflakes were slicing into his eyeballs. He couldn't locate where the voice was coming from.

"Hey, over here, big man, to the right, behind you."

Kweku turned and saw a man waving an arm out of a door ten metres behind him, the way he'd come. The voice he'd heard made him pretty sure he was Ghanaian too.

"Ah, man, finally. HE HE."

Kweku's booming voice and laugh echoed between the buildings. He moved in the direction of the man's silhouette, as fast as he could, but carefully too, to not fall.

"Ah, I did not see you."

The man was about the same size as Kweku.

"Where you come from? Is that a dead man on your shoulder?"

"Not dead. Hurt. You from Ghana?"

"Yes man, Ghana, and you?"

"Ghana too."

"So no dead man?"

"No no. No dead man. Just out cold. Can we come in? I work at the church. Up the hill. Night-man. He hit his head on the stairs. Been out cold, maybe half an hour now. Can we come in? You night-man too?"

"Yes, night-man, yes yes, come in."

The man took a step backwards, and as Kweku passed him, Wolfgang's feet kicked him in the stomach. His suit-jacket was dirtied. He smiled and shook his head.

"Straight on, let me lock up and follow you."

Kweku stood in what had to be a lobby. There were stairs going up and down on his right and a corridor going ahead. A large ornamental plaque was covering the main wall, two dragons either side of a flag he didn't know but guessed was the red cross of the Red Cross. He started down the dark corridor. There was a light at the end, from within a room whose door was half-closed. It looked a bit creepy. His shoes went squueekk squuueekk on the hard linoleum. He heard his fellow Ghanaian rattle his keys and slam the outer door close. A draft stopped.

"In that door, yes. Good."

Kweku pushed through. In the room there was a bed.

"Yes, yes, put him there, that's right, on the bed. No need to take off the shoes."

The fellow night watchman had caught up and was

standing behind Kweku, filling the frame of the door. Kweku lumped Wolfgang onto the bed, as carefully as he could. He was starting to feel so tired he was contemplating laying down for a few moments too. To catch his breath. But he didn't. Instead he praised his magnet as he straightened up.

"What is this place?"

"A school. You do not know it?"

"No."

"Where you from in Ghana?"

"Accra."

"Good. Accra too."

The man was familiar-looking. Like Kweku's, his voice came from deep down within him. It was hoarse, faint and booming all at the same time.

"When did you come here?"

"You mean England?

"Yes."

"This year, eight months. And you?

"Me too my friend. What is your name?"

"Kweku."

"Kweku, my name is Kwame."

He extended his hand and Kweku shook it.

"You say he is out cold? How long?"

"Yes. He fell, and then he fell again, on the church floor."

"Ah, so he fell twice? As we say, no pain no gain my friend."

Kweku nodded and looked at Wolfgang. It was like he was sleeping now. Resting. Not being hurt or knocked out at all.

"Kwame, is this normal weather here in England?"

"I don't know. That is why I was out looking. That is how I saw you my friend. Let me call an ambulance."

He lifted the receiver.

"Damn. No signal."

Kweku was getting worried. His magnet had given no indication that this was a bad snow, unusual. But then again maybe it had been too focused on getting him there? Maybe. And what about this man? What was wrong with him? He'd never seen anyone out cold this long.

"So bad snow is how bad Kwame? Is it permanent?"

Kwame sat down in the only chair in the small room. There was no window to the outside. Kweku was sitting on the bed with Wolfgang's feet in his lap.

"Ah. I do not know for certain Kweku, but permanent is a relative thing in most cases. Would you not say?"

"I suppose you are right."

"For instance, this summer I believed that the rain was permanent. Now I know that three months is not permanent, not here, but after two months and a few days it can seem that way."

Kweku nodded. His face was warm. He passed a weary hand over it. He was feeling more and more worried.

"But how you know then Kwame that this is such a bad snow? It has only snowed for maybe half a day?"

"Very true my friend. But I did not say the snow was permanent. You asked me that. I only said that permanent is relative. Did you go to the university Kweku?"

Kwame picked up the receiver again. Still no signal.

"Yes I did. Two years in Accra. Now I go here."

"How old are you Kweku?"

"Twenty-eight."

"Listen Kweku."

Kwame was leaning forward in his seat. He held his two hands together, not gesturing or moving them much about. His speech was not hurried. He wasn't moving his arse about looking for a comfortable position.

"I know this much about the world. It is a place with much force and much we do not know. So Kweku, you come on to the step of the church and you see this man in the snow, and you take him in and he fell again, on the church floor?"

"Yes."

"And then you carry him here, in the snow, but you did not know I was here? You did not know this place even at all, did you?"

Kweku shook his head.

"No. So, you have only been here eight months my friend, like me, and still you find me here on a night like this, so I ask you Kweku, did you ever in your life feel like this before, like you did tonight? Did you ever feel destiny as you did tonight? Did you ever feel it pull as hard as tonight? I ask you my friend, is it maybe not a strange snow?"

"Yes."

"OK. But now look at him now, this man, we do not know who he is. Does he look to you like a man out cold? No. He looks like a man to me, like he is asleep. So I say, when I think about the snow and about you coming here Kweku, and this sleeping man that won't wake up, is it not an exstraordinary night in the world to be so accidental?"

"Yes."

"Yes, a strange night Kweku. This man seems to be smiling and dreaming sweet. Have you felt his pulse?"

"No."

Kwame leant over and held Wolfgang's wrist. Then he nodded and pulled the edges of his mouth down into a satisfied expression.

"OK. Still alive."

He lifted the receiver, but there was no signal.

Wolfgang's hand slumped slowly onto the bed, as if somehow he was controlling it.

"By the way Kweku, what is your wage up there in the church on the hill?"

"They pay the minimum one."

"OK Listen. This is what we do."

/>

<biography

Kweku Agbenyega (née Edem), born 1989, Accra, Ghana, father unknown, mother deceased 1993, adopted by his uncle and aunt, mistreated, ran away, became a resident at the Kaneshie home for boys in 1995, received special attention by the boys home's highly spiritual caretaker, Kwasi Agbenyega (of the Ewé people), played up front for the home's football team, scored consistently, adopted by said Kwasi Agbenyega and his wife Abra in 1997, received home-schooling by Abra, along with her and Kwasi's five children (subjects included arithmetic, reading and writing, rhetoric, history, spirituality, music, football), showed great interest in understanding the relation in Ewé religion between drumming and destiny, discovered he had a good head, worked nights at a local gas station saving money for his further education, enrolled at the Knutsford University College, Accra, for a BSc in Business Administration (General Management), met a university recruiter from the UK, had no reason to distrust his offer to study at Oxford University, left Accra and entered the UK on a six months language school visa he was told would be upgraded upon expiration, paid for his own flight, before leaving paid £3,578 by money transfer to the London Oxford Institute, upon exiting immigration and customs was not met as agreed, took the Piccadilly Line to Green Park where he walked around looking for an affordable hotel but couldn't find one, asked for directions to the London Oxford Institute on Hackney Road, went there and sat outside the entrance all night, was enrolled the next day, told he could find accommodation in a house owned by the institute on Mare Street, told he could work nights at St. Paul's Cathedral to meet his living expenses, sought out the Ghanaian High Commission in London and hung around the driver's quarters, making friends with the High Commissioner's personal chauffeur, realised he'd been thoroughly conned, also realised he had no legal protection, decided to stay in London nonetheless (he had no money for a return-ticket as he'd been promised a scholarship at Oxford University), thought he'd better make the best of it, focused on what Kwasi had taught him about destiny, spent a lot of time thinking about what had happened to him, did not become bitter but became quiet and remote and dreamy, started developing some theories of his own, about the way things hung together, remembered an old tale Kwasi had told him about magnets, how invisible magnets pulled us along, thought the idea made sense, sat late at night in St. Paul's cathedral thinking about the theory of magnets, developed it considerably, experienced a prolonged period of melancholia pondering his past and where he was now and what to do with himself if the theory of magnets was correct, which didn't make him less dreamy, which made his eyes increasingly sad-looking, felt lonely and abandoned, considered converting to Christianity and joining the church-band as their drummer, but didn't, heard one evening a voice screaming outside the cathedral doors, went out to see what was going on, saw that it had been snowing, saw that it was still snowing, heard the screaming again and went towards the sound, through the snow, found a man on the ground, lifted him up and brought him into the cathedral, experienced the man loosing consciousness, twice, decided to take him somewhere to get help, made it through multiple complications and thick falling snow to St. Thomas' hospital, a few weeks later sought out the man's flatmates, was served a coffee while he told the story of how Wolfgang had fallen off his bike and was brought to the hospital, was thanked heartily and offered to stay the night, accepted the offer as it was now snowing so much he would never get home, was introduced to the Mayor of London whom he found cold and distracted, was introduced to a warm-hearted woman in her sixties called Liv Olsen, from Norway, was offered an important job as part of her team, accepted the offer and was given the title Chief Snow Removal Officer (CSRO), was happy he could be of service, was astonished by the way his life was changing.

/>

/operation_snow_removal

Started at Sat Sep 16 04:46:28 27020

Command line was: ./henkick_1262 --out-dir=store/
final_rebuild --out-postfix=arx_run_0_no_clean
--creat-sigma=10 --no-plot --save-plot --kwg-
base=hk_kwg_9.db --drives-list=drives.txt --drive-
idx=101

Version tag 3.12.1.1262, built Sat Sep 16 04:46:25
27020

Job ID is: 267391, 1402 instances allocated

VC hash: 6a3b499fac87

parsing recovered files at /store/recovery/
drvU5D

<the_key_objectives

Unusually hung-over, Bjørn's mother Liv pondered the extent of her task from the cab of the chained-up tractor. Kweku, her driver and right-hand man, was quietly concentrating, making sure they didn't knock down too many signs or lights. Her arms were aching dully, persistently. It was still snowing, of course.

It had been a mistake finishing that bottle of vodka after Bjørn had passed out. Now her thoughts were appearing in her mind like little bubbles floating up from a crab on the bottom of the sea. Her mouth tasted like a mix of old bloody mucus and a cold herbal infusion.

Her meeting was at 10 a.m. down on Victoria Embankment, just below Temple station. She had demanded the Mayor bring all the GLA staff he could get hold of, particularly anyone with good knowledge of the Thames, its tidal fluctuations and relative depths. She had told the Norwegian Ambassador to be there too, just to keep him busy. Kweku had said the Ghanaian High Commissioner was a dependable guy, so she'd had him summoned as well.

Her key objectives were to build a core team she could trust, find suitable dumping spots; then get recruiting for drivers for her fleet of equipment still left up in Harwich. She knew Kirsty and Bjørn could do the public relations bit, as long as she kept them on a tight leash. At least she trusted them, and the media were more or less crippled anyway, without broadband access.

From her elevated vantage point in the tractor she saw the street-wide desolation. Snow had blown up against buildings in strange formations owing to the wind patterns created around skyscrapers. A lot of shops and ground-floor businesses had been broken into, their giant windowpanes hanging perforated from being hit by bricks, or cracked like old porcelain glazing from stray gunshots. The swirling yellow light from the safety-warning bulb on the tractor's roof shone feebly in the buildings' marble and stone facades.

Going down Eastcheap she caught the reflection of herself sitting behind Kweku in one of the few unbroken windows they passed. She thought she looked massive, like a bear riding on the shoulders of a man riding a small motorbike. When had she become so big? As if she'd turned into another person without her noticing? And now this person was here, filling up space in this tractor? About to start a job that would potentially require a younger woman's health and energy. A stamina she'd once had, last time she'd been called up, back in Oslo in the eighties. Now she remembered how tough that had actually been. How taxing, both mentally and physically. It felt like her former body, the younger one, the one inside this added flesh, was reminding her of its previous ordeals, testing and teasing her, ridiculing this later blown-up incarnation, sapping her of self-confidence. But why would her own body be against her? Her own past? She looked ahead at the snow-covered street, at the signs of the random human destruction. A burnt-out car wreck was smouldering still, left inexplicably leaning against a lamp-post, covering over by snow. She felt a tautness settling into her throat and jaw, then a real stinging pain, a jab of pure doubt perhaps, and she grabbed hold of Kweku's jacket at the back.

He stopped the tractor and turned around.

"Are you OK?"

His worried stare woke her to herself. She nodded and let go of the jacket.

"Yes, I am OK. Sorry. It was nothing. Just a…"

The tractor's engine was idling loudly, their voices barely reaching above the din.

"I think I understand," Kweku said. "This won't be easy right? Big responsibility for you?"

She smiled a melancholy smile.

"Yes. No. I don't think it will be easy. But someone has got to..."

Her sentence trailed off as she turned around to see how Bjørn was doing, towed on his skis behind them, connected with a rope tied around his waist. He seemed to be doing fine despite throwing up for an hour before setting off. She thought they ought to cut down on their drinking. If they wanted to survive more than a month like this. She had a job to do and would make sure she did it to the best of her ability.

/>

<documentation

When the dumping-plan was agreed (parks, major inner-urban undeveloped areas, abandoned council estates, the entire Olympic Park, the Thames and its estuary) and the big machines came rolling in (the noise becoming deafening), Bjørn's task changed to skiing around on his own and reporting back on progress.

As he did his documentation, snapping away with his digital camera, he felt increasingly puzzled by what he was seeing, and not just by the collapse of infrastructure, the looting and the general state of emergency, but from looking at the actual things, really looking for once, at the parts; the doork nobs and door handles, the windows, the awnings; the stone, bronze and marble monuments; the different-coloured bricks, the lamp-posts, the mazes of scaffolding; the stuff the city consisted of, piece by piece, layer by layer. And he remembered his gnawing, almost humming realisation up around Romford, when he'd seen the city from a distance (in that stark light) and had felt it communicating something he didn't quite get. He remembered he'd sensed the first of it then, this obsession with his physical surroundings. And as he kept looking, kept snapping pictures and skiing around everywhere on his own, he'd started getting what the stuff was saying.

And what was it saying?

Let's go by way of example: picture him standing in Piccadilly Circus. It could've been roughly mid-day on a Tuesday, almost four months into the snowstorm. The light would've been an even white, dispersing through the cloud and the falling snow. He wouldn't have been able to see the sun, couldn't have seen what direction the light was coming from. He would've had his skis on his feet, his poles stuck into the snow either side of him. He would've been looking through the viewfinder of his digital SLR. He would've taken his gloves off to be able to operate the small buttons, the dials. He would've been taking a picture of the large iconic curving advertising wall, the one with the TDK, SANYO, Coca-Cola, McDonald's and SAMSUNG ads, except they wouldn't be there anymore, flashing, changing, illuminating. The wall would be black. Its electricity switched off. Instead he would've seen a number of dull dark surfaces, studded with thousands of small glass bulbs. He would've been able to see this because he was zooming in. He would've pressed the shutter-release. Taking the camera away from his eyes, he would've looked at the wall he remembered so well from pictures and postcards, from coming here now and then, from passing through, and he would've seen its uniform blackness.

But he would still remember the lights. His memory would still have been able to produce the ads.

Around him the snowploughs would've been loudly grinding their noses into the curbs. He would've registered that the wall and its constituent parts had at least two qualities, one as individual part, one as part of a whole. He would've registered that they were never just one of these things, but always both at the same time. The formerly lit up billboards were a part of the square, a part of his soup of memories, the square a part of London, connected by streets and tunnels to other parts.

He would've looked away from the darkened billboard and focused on the lamp-posts scattered about him. The bulbs in the lamps would've been unlit. He would've thought about the connecting cables in the ground running from one lamp-post to the next. But mostly he would've thought about the design, repeated with modifications around town, depending on how old they were; the choice of material, the clear and not so clear artistic influences (Greek columns, Etruscan sarcophagi). He would've registered intent beyond the functional one, beyond randomness. He would've seen and heard a human urge to express something.

He would've turned around to avoid the snow falling into his eyes and he would've looked at the shop windows of the GAP, almost all smashed in. He would've noticed the way the windows had been secured to the metal frame when they were there. He would've looked at the shop next door, a large Boots, and would've noticed how the shattered glass doors were once connected to the concrete walls either side. He would've registered the colour of putty used, or thought that this was perhaps a PWC window fitting. He would've thought about what putty was made of. What PWC was. He would've asked himself: Who makes putty? PWC? Where? In Malaysia? Would it be snowing there too?

Perhaps initially, as he'd started out on his observations, he would've thought about the things around him, the individual bricks, the thousands of street-signs, the tiny bulbs in the darkened billboards, like individual indifferent atoms. But gradually, as he was spending more and more time skiing around town on his own, looking more and more intently, he would've perhaps also thought that these atoms fired up a longing human universe. That there was a connection. And for a while he would've stood looking, observing, and the snow would've started settling on his shoulders, and he would've felt uneasy, a sense of having somehow been wrong about something important settling into his abdomen.

/>

＜recruiting_drive

The Wolfgang Ender Memorial HQ, Shadwell, East London, formerly just Wolfgang, the Dane and Bjørn's apartment. The stylised Warholesque picture of Wolfgang made by the Dane hung on the entrance door, making it clear what apartment to head for in order to submit your application and sit for your interview for one of the many hundreds of snow-removal jobs just advertised on lamp-posts all over town. Though, you didn't need the picture of Wolfgang to show you the way, the queue was snaking along the corridor down the stairs, out into the lobby, past the hall, through the main entrance, along the pavement to the left, down through Watney Market in a zigzag pattern, in-between the stalls selling products that shouldn't really be frozen, out onto Commercial Road, down towards Whitechapel as far as the eye could see in the snowy mist.

Kweku stood at the entrance to the apartment with an old-fashioned clipboard taking names and noting down any kind of identification number being produced: old passports, the long number on the front of a loyalty card for Sainsbury's, the almost invisible numbers under the barcode on a Fitness First membership card, you name it, library-cards, coffee-shop loyalty cards; all kinds of certificates of authentication, NHS cards, inoculation cards, really any kind of card or scrap of paper that would allow Kweku to identify this person as one, and only one unique individual.

He took digital snaps of each person holding their I.D. next to their face. Quite often he took pictures of someone's tattoo as well, if it wasn't too hard to get to or too privately placed (with the chosen piece of I.D. in the frame). He noted down stated as well as presumed nationality to be able to group the various teams once members had been hired, for language reasons mostly, but also to avoid ethnic tension when strictly speaking there was enough to get on with already. He noticed a lot of Ghanaians which pleased him, lots of West-Africans in general, though the Somali were also showing strong, and the Spanish, the Greek, the Turks, the Kurds, the Polish, the Chinese, the Asian community

[sic], even English people, people from Wales, even Ireland. Briefly put, more or less every kind of nationality under the once visible sun. Though he noted the absence of Swedes, the Swiss (from all three parts) and Italians.

Once the men and women had been identified, and their turn was up, Kweku pointed them in the direction of the closed living room door, wishing them a cordial 'good luck with it', telling them to knock quietly.

On the other side of the living room door Liv was seated heavily at the rickety IKEA dining table, formerly desk, with a mug of coffee in her hand and a large map of London spread out before her. She was facing the door. Her hair was all over the place from having worn a hat that morning. Above the door hung Wolfgang's old windsurf board, still, a dampening heavy presence, a reminder of happier, care-freer times, making the prospective snow-removers' entrance to the living room feel really claustrophobic and nerve-racking. Despite Liv's insistence on improved cleanliness, the room still smelled both damp and dusty. Behind the kitchen-bar-cum-worktop-cum-overflowing-shelf for innumerable unnameable objects, stood Bjørn, ready to assist his mother should this become necessary. He was wearing his skier-outfit, a pair of glasses made for low contrast conditions. They turned his blue eyes green in the light of the long-life light bulb. On the side of the table facing the large floor-to-ceiling windows (the room's only saving grace), the Mayor reclined in Roman fashion on the gigantic beanbag that had also once belonged to Wolfgang. Behind his apple-shaped head the snow was falling slowly but steadily. He'd said he just wanted to see a few candidates, to know what was going on. To see how Liv managed things. What her emphasis was. What kind of people she was employing for him. He'd felt the need to make that clear. He'd felt his authority wasn't exactly where and what it should be. He'd felt it slipping away. He'd felt that Liv was maybe even a tougher cookie than advertised. Really actually mostly felt like going home and watching a stack of DVDs. Really, if he was to be completely honest for once, couldn't get himself to do anything sensible anymore. He had no plan for what to do when he woke up in the morning. No urge to get out of bed. He felt his ability to just function, sort of normally, slipping away. He felt himself marginalised, really. That's what it was. The apathy. He was out there offstage watching the play from between the curtains. He couldn't really mobilise any energy to fight this growing feeling of uselessness. He kept trying to find phone reception. He wondered if he was turning a critical bend on the mental-sanity-map. To a place very few people ever came back from. He found himself daydreaming more and more – about things he wished he'd done, different careers, something more artistic. Childhood memories were coming back to him with increasing clarity. A layer of melancholy added for each one he relived. A growing sadness he couldn't shake. Enveloping him. He looked out the window at the falling snowflakes and sighed.

Liv had made it clear she wanted no interference. Whatsoever. The Norwegian Ambassador had already been told to take a long hard walk, his vacuous smile getting on her tits, his slimy friendliness throwing up itchy rashes on everyone's necks, the Mayor's included.

A prospective hiree knocked. Liv shouted: "come in!"

As the elderly person entered there was close to absolute silence in the room. He shut the squeaking door behind him, walked across the fake parquet floor under the shadow of the surfboard, stopped hesitantly by the stool at the table where Liv sat, clutched his hat. The Mayor scratched his arse and checked his phone. Bjørn absentmindedly searched his beard for an old pimple.

"Please sit down," she said. "You do not need to be worried."

The Slavic-looking man took a seat on the stool and almost fell off it, backwards. His arms grabbed hopelessly at the stuffy air.

"Driver's licence?"

"Yes," he said, short of breath, not really knowing what he'd been asked.

"What type?"

"Yes."

"Car?"

"Yes."

He smiled at Liv and she smiled back, making him feel a bit more at ease, though his head was wearily twisting from over by the windows and the Mayor, to over by the kitchen and Bjørn.

"Tractor?"

"Yes."

"Good. So we can start you working a snowplough then, if you have got tractor experience, OK?"

"...?"

"OK?"

"Yes, OK... OK." He nodded vigorously and smiled a brown-toothed smile. The Mayor stirred, as if to say something, but Liv lifted a hand without looking at him, and the Mayor lay back down again.

"Where are you from?"

"...?"

"Country? Home?"

"Ah, domo... Kiev," he said, happily. The memory of the place seemed to momentarily lift his spirits.

"Very very snow. Kiev. Very very."

"Good."

"Yes, good, Kiev very very good."

"Chicken Kiev," the Mayor muttered to himself.

The man looked rapidly his way but Liv drew him back.

"Pay no attention. So can you start today?"

"...?"

"Today..." She tapped her right index's nail on the tabletop.

"Start...?" She did the classic black-and-white-Hollywood-as-if-she-was-driving movement. It pained her arms. She grinned. The elderly wrinkled man smiled a wide encouraging smile and nodded.

"OK. Good. You start today." She made a note on the paper laid on top of the map before her.

"Yes, " he answered, smiling.

"Thank you."

"Yes."

"Bjørn, can you show him out? And tell Kweku he is a B6?"

"Sure."

Bjørn motioned the small elderly man from the stool. And getting up he smiled, bowed, and Liv smiled back, waving slightly with her right arm, and the man folded his hands and moved them up and down in front of him as he turned around to face the surfboard, the corridor, the exit.

"spasybi..." he said, "spasybi." And was led out.

/>

<update

The small living room in Shadwell had long since turned into a makeshift operations centre. Messages and orders were sent out, status reports were brought back. Kweku was coordinating the snow-moving-machinery shift-work from Wolfgang's empty room. Bjørn's mother was making some ersatz coffee and checking the latest weather reports. Around town her plan was being carried out. The large yellow machines were shovelling. The equally large and yellow dumpers were dumping the snow where agreed. The noise was terrific, deafening. It was still snowing, heavily.

Collective action. Coordinated passion for those with less ability. Fewer means. Bjørn's mother had been pulling out the old social democratic rhetoric. There had even been whispers, comparisons to world historical leaders:

Churchill, Nelson Mandela, Joan of Arc, even a Nobel Price (but in what?). The Mayor was sitting in the corner fiddling with his phone, wearing an old tracksuit and wool-lined wellingtons, sulking, sighing, giving Liv tough but ultimately pathetic looks.

Bjørn's mother had taught the public relations industry a few lessons too. People from various agencies had been over several times to observe her work. It wasn't enough to have the theory down, they realised. You needed to carry through under pressure. To stay authentic. To not sell out. To not paint it too rosy or too bleak. To be realistic, basically. People liked honesty, particularly when it was delivered in a quirky Norwegian accent by an older woman with heaps of natural charisma, the old-school matron-way; a mother-figure.

At night the core team ate together, huddled around the wobbly IKEA desk in the former living room. Everyone was downbeat, so they didn't talk much. The meals, so-called comfort food, were sourced locally, from the Bangladeshi stores mostly, sacks of flour and rice, tubs of oil, dried fruits, dried fish, turned into fragrant curries, but it didn't make them feel any better.

Recently all the city's park vehicles were rounded up and repurposed, some for simple shuttle-traffic, some for elderly taxi-service, wherever there was a need and the streets had been kept relatively snow-free. Down by the Thames the mountains of snow were stopping you from seeing the south-bank, or the north-bank, depending. One couldn't just drop it all in at the same time, the water needed to be kept ice-free. That was a challenge. All around town there were snowmen made to look like the Mayor, the freaky hair quite well reproduced by all kinds of frozen vegetables stuck into a massive white head.

Down on Watney Market the stalls were being erected as per usual, almost. They'd had some problems making the metal structures stable on ice. Fruit peel, packaging, general trash and other more unusual stuff had in places become veritable killing traps of slipperiness. Older ladies were often seen horizontal, first in the air, then on the ground, a weird kind of acceptance in their falls, like trees falling alone in the forest.

Over by the Bleeding Heart a fake-DVD vendor had her work cut out trying to extricate the thin plastic-sleeves from the ice. She was using a crème brûlée burner, slowly, inch by inch, leaving a glassy surface, as she didn't want to scorch the damn things. At one moment the rectangle area looked like some animator's idea of an ice-age vending machine, some sort of cover-flow for cavemen.

About sixty bits of torn paper on the side of the market's obligatory eel and pie van was asking if someone had seen so and so pet, gone for the last week or two. The sad-looking pets in the photographs were staring out into the falling snow. Over by the library a few crows were pecking at a bunch of frozen bananas, colour beautifully intact, no brown blemishes whatsoever. How long had they been there? When a particularly strong gust of wind swept along the ground, the frozen jackets, shirts and dresses, hung up on the metal-rails, moved like loose barrels on deck in a storm. At some point a six-year old boy had been caught between two separated sections of fake Boss jackets and had been knocked unconscious, pale and bleeding. The light fluffy fluttering of saris and chiffon cloth was definitely nowhere to be seen. A lot of the kids were shutting up for once too, due to the swelling of sore tongues. Licking frozen metal was why. It was oddly quiet for that reason.

/>

<what_was_that_again?

Sitting at the large conference table in his suite at the Russell hotel the Mayor checked his phone. Nothing. Two minutes later he checked it again. Still nothing. He looked across the table at the Norwegian Ambassador; saw him checking his phone as well. Nothing coming through there either it seemed.

"Nothing?"

"No. Nothing."

"Yeah. Same here."

He checked it again just to be sure. Nothing. Just the picture of his wife wearing a bikini on a beach on the island of Lombok, as wallpaper. In the upper right-hand corner: a lower-case x where there should've been an ascending bar-chart indicating signal strength. In the upper left-hand corner: a graphic element indicating battery-life, the white supine rectangle one-third full with white. The relative fullness of the battery-icon was a source of feeling momentarily OK.

They were waiting for Liv and Kweku to arrive, maybe also the Ghanaian High Commissioner, whose presence had been requested by Liv, but passively-aggressively opposed by himself and the Norwegian Ambassador. He checked his phone again. Nothing. He pressed the phone's button with an upwards backwards-turned arrow on it. The display lit up. Nothing. He looked at the Norwegian Ambassador who'd also just checked his phone and caught his eyes.

"...?"

"Nah. Nothing. And you?

"No. Nothing."

Looking down again he checked his phone one more time, just out of deeply ingrained habit (nothing) and decided to put it back in his trouser-pocket. For a few seconds he felt good about having been so decisive about getting it out of view. Then he thought that maybe it could've caught a signal just as he put it away, so he got it out again and checked it once more. Nothing. Just to make sure he wouldn't forget his password he pressed the 'unlock' button and entered it (a combination usually rated as 'weak' or 'insecure' by most password protected sites and devices).

He locked the phone as soon as it had been unlocked, and this time he put it in his jacket's inner breast pocket, the jacket hanging on the next chair.

It felt risky – it didn't feel good at all to have it so far away. He took it back out again and put it on the table in front of him, but now with the display down. He'd put it on vibrate so he'd feel it, most likely hear it. He took a shallow breath through his nose, blew it out straightway, then rested his arms either side of the phone and his note-pad, for no more than five seconds, before he turned to his briefcase by his chair's left leg and took out a tablet computer which cover he expertly flipped over onto the back, to form its rest. Then he placed the whole thing like a miniature skateboard-ramp in front of him on the table.

He pushed the 'on' button. From sleep-mode the device took no time at all to react. It showed no reception. He sighed. Where were Liv and Kweku? He looked at his wristwatch although he'd checked the digitally displayed watches on both his phone and his tablet just seconds ago. It took him a little while to reconcile the analogue information with what he'd just seen displayed digitally. It was more or less the same. The wristwatch was a fraction late, which made him feel instant dislike towards it. He shook his arm to make the feeling of being dirtied by the watch go away.

Then he felt a daydream coming on, a slackening of tension. He saw himself up on stage playing an important role in a Shakespeare play, delivering a difficult soliloquy, *to be or not to be*? No. It had to be King Lear, towards the end of the play. Yes. That was more like it. He felt the dignity of doing this, the admiration of the crowd. It felt like it was warming him from inside. He looked out at the audience through the glare of the spotlights. They were giving him a standing ovation, one that grew more and more intense. Whistles. Shouts of HURRAH. He smiled humbly, honoured, feeling goose bumps ripple down his neck. Then there was the after-party, at the Ivy, red Bordeaux and filets of Cordon Bleu, stiff white napkins, everyone around the table complementing him, touching him admiringly. Cutlery clinking. A wonderful buzz in the restaurant. He thanked them each and one in a sincere manner, holding every smiling gaze fast with his open and honest eyes, feeling intensely humble and thankful for being in such unmannered, appreciative, yes, cultured company.

He checked his phone again (nothing) and put it a little further away on the table, but decided to bring it closer. He sat back in the creaky arm-rested chair and opened his eyes wide, breathing audibly through his nose. Outside the hotel-suite's large floor-to-ceiling windows the snow was falling with what would be considered a cosy romantic quality had it not been snowing constantly like that for months. The Norwegian Ambassador checked his phone. The Mayor did too.

"…?"

"Nope."

"Yep. Same here."

They both sighed loudly and shook their heads.

"What time is it?"

The Mayor checked his phone, then his wristwatch, then his tablet.

"Eleven forty-three… forty-four," he said, looking at all three time-keeping devices simultaneously. The Norwegian Ambassador checked his phone too.

"You're right," he said. "They're late."

The Mayor took off his wristwatch and put it in his briefcase.

"Yes, they are."

He swore he would never wear it again.

"How much longer should we wait?" the Ambassador asked.

"Well, what else can we do?"

"That's true." The Ambassador looked towards the snow beyond the window. "You're right."

They both checked their phones again. Someone knocked but they didn't react.

After a while the maid's head appeared in-between the door and the wall.

"Yes?" the Mayor said.

"Oh, sorry," the maid said and withdrew, closing the door. The Mayor and the Ambassador looked at each other and shook their heads. Then they checked their phones again.

After what felt like twenty minutes, but was more like five, the Ghanaian High Commissioner quietly entered the room, followed by Kweku and Bjørn's mother Liv, all three brushing large quantities of snow from their all-weather clothes. The Mayor and the Norwegian Ambassador, both busy looking at something important on their phones, did not greet them. As the three newly-arrived got ready to sit down, the Mayor finally looked up and feigned a mild surprise at not having heard them enter. He looked at his watchless wrist; pulled a grimace indicating he'd forgot something.

"Reception up again?" Liv asked, looking at their phones.

"Eh? Oh..." The Mayor looked at his phone. "No. Just some old emails."

"Yes, old emails," the Ambassador said.

Liv nodded. "I see."

She sat down. Kweku and the Ghanaian High Commissioner also sat down. The High Commissioner took out his phone.

"What else have you been doing this morning?" Liv asked.

The Mayor looked at the Ambassador who was busy checking his phone again. She let her eyes quizzically pass between them. The mayor put his tablet back in the briefcase by his left foot, then changed his mind and took it out again, placing it, without flipping the cover open, to the left of his phone and his note-pad.

"OK," Liv said, looking at Kweku and the High Commissioner. "Let's get started now, shall we? Kweku, can you give us an update on removal?"

"Certainly." He looked down on his scribbled notes. "Let us see then... All operational vehicles deployed, north and south today, fourteen drivers ill with the flu, five concussed, major blockages on the Strand... We need more drivers really, is what I'm saying..."

He continued reading from his notes for a good five minutes, giving the Mayor and the Ambassador ample opportunity to check their phones several times as well as get more and more distracted by the way the falling snowflakes outside the window seemed to swirl around exactly one horizontal rotation just before they each settled on the snow below.

"Thanks Kweku," Liv said when he had finished.

"Gentlemen, any questions?"

They shook their heads.

"High Commissioner?"

The High Commissioner, a tall lanky man, looked up, shook his head, putting aside his phone. "Nope."

"OK. Then what about fuel? What Kweku said about our current fuel levels? No questions about that? Comments? Suggestions?"

The three men shook their heads in silence, looking down.

"Nope, that's all good," the Mayor said.

"So running out of fuel in roughly four weeks is OK? Most likely sooner? Which is not only a problem for our vehicles... But you realise people will start freezing? That's OK with you?"

"What was that?" the Mayor said, looking at his phone.

"The fuel situation," Liv said.

"What about it?" the Mayor said, still looking at his phone.

"Were you listening to what Kweku said just now? Either of you?"

Kweku looked anxiously at Liv. She wasn't happy at all. She was getting weak. Losing her colour. Her wit. Her magnet was most certainly flagging.

The Mayor put his phone down for a moment and looked at Liv.

"Sorry, what was that again?"

/>

<something_heavy

Bjørn was alone in the apartment, standing in the living room, looking out the floor-to-ceiling windows. His day had been spent documenting a special situation down in Greenwich, an area unfortunately neglected for weeks. It hadn't looked good – not at all. A month and a half ago a couple of the largest dumpers brought down from Norway had crashed on the high-street, close to Cutty Sark, lodging themselves into the buildings on opposite sides of the one-way system, forming a perfect barricade. Absolutely immobile. Unless dynamite was an option, which they'd decided against for fear of producing a landslide into the Thames.

Only a week later and the dumpers were invisible, just a white wall between the buildings either side. This sublime barrier had thrown a ripple-effect-type spanner into the whole of the south-east London operations, shutting down ploughing routes and dumping spots in a wide radius, forcing Liv's open-eyed and tactical neglect of that part of town, letting the whole place simply fight for itself – a fight it became obvious was way beyond doomed, the citizens up and leaving in a steady treacle as the hopelessness dawned on them, trudging their way in a long line down the single existing path out of there.

Most of these people had disappeared west and south then, into the snowdrift, to whoever knew where and what, leaving Kweku and his team of volunteers the task of evacuating and re-housing the few left behind, the ones not able to move themselves or just stubbornly holding on.

Staring out the apartment's window, thinking about his day, his mind uneasily drifting, Bjørn suddenly saw the jagged spikes of a lightning-bolt. Its bright light instantly turning the falling uniformity of snowflakes into a matrix of singular dark silhouettes, bringing home the unimaginable number of crystals that were actually coming down to earth at any time.

He instinctively started counting the seconds to the first roar of thunder, the way his father had taught him. It arrived at two, making the windows vibrate. Two times three hundred and forty metres per second meant the lightning had materialised roughly seven hundred metres away, or up above. Another blindingly bright zap followed, and another count to two, and it felt like the house was about to give in to the shockwave of sound. Bjørn had never heard anything like it. It was terrifying. Immediately another zap forked aggressively into the whiteness, seemingly striking the helicopter landing-pad on top of Whitechapel hospital. There was no need to count the seconds. The thunderclap was almost instantaneous. In the peculiar clarity created by the light and the sound, Bjørn thought he saw the snowflakes move up a bit, and then down, before they resumed normal falling, as if someone had cued the scene back and forth on a timeline.

Bjørn staggered backwards away from the window, the sound of the thunder rolling on like fighter-jets flying low in disparate directions. The whole thing felt so shockingly out of place in prosaic Shadwell. Like a lesson of truth intended for a different geological age. What next? Something fittingly epic? Prehistoric? Something mushroom-formed? As if a meteor had struck nearby? A volcano stirred into eruption? That the Whitechapel hospital would spontaneously combust in an ultraviolet blaze?

But nothing happened. The bolts of lightning grew fewer and further apart, and the seconds till each successive thunder extended, until he eventually couldn't hear them anymore. He moved up to the windowpane again, observing the last flickers of distant lighting moving away into the whiteness, like retorts come too late. Then the snowflakes fell quietly and eternally again, the daylight starting to slip into the blue before darkness.

The air in the cluttered living room felt unbearably stale all of a sudden. Immobile. Like it was sapping his strength to simply breath it in. Where was the room's oxygen coming from anyway? It had been impossible to open the windows for months. The relatively new apartment was appallingly ventilated. What was the effect of so much snow on the make up of the atmosphere? Was oxygen running out more generally? Now that they would most likely be skipping spring?

He put a hand on the window, steadying himself. It was much cooler than he'd expected. He suddenly felt exhausted. He'd been going on reserves for way too long and only now realised. A little damp formed on the glass around his fingers. He removed his hand and saw its outline left behind, before it quickly evaporated. He needed to rest. He felt dizzy.

He lay down on the beanbag and closed his eyes. After a while a static kind of silence filled his ears and his consciousness drifted between what felt like darker and lighter bumps and hollows in his mind. He thought about

the static sound as the lack of oxygen in the air, as maybe
the sound of snowflakes colliding, landing and piling up on
the balcony just beyond the large floor-to-ceiling windows
to his right.

Then he started dreaming a vivid, half lucid
dream. He was aware of his position as the dreamer
lying on the beanbag, the objects surrounding him in
the room, encircled by different scenes of action, one in
which a transparent version of his body, seen from his
reclined beanbag dreamers position, was filling up with
snowflakes, the snow only falling within the outline of
his body, making him feel like coughing, like he was
losing his breath. Next to this scene he felt he saw his
mother and the Mayor making love in the middle of a
large football stadium, full to capacity, the crowd cheering
them on, shouting out names of positions they wanted
to see adopted, his beanbag floating nearby, above a
concession stand where people were busy buying sticks
of dynamite that looked like hot-dogs. Next to this scene,
like further into the dream, he saw Wolfgang and the
Dane carrying back to the apartment the various objects
that were already there, as if they were fulfilling these
objects' raison d'être by finally adding in the Aristotelian
soul, the Anima, the aspect that would make these things
capable of realising their potential. And as each object

was added back to the apartment, fusing with the already existing counterpart in the room, each of these things started to dance and swirl around in the air, each proclaiming their essential quality. The spare bicycle-tire said: personal freedom! The long discarded DVD player jollily proclaimed: home entertainment! A floating cluster of spare IKEA-furniture-nuts-and-bolts groaned: ah... frustration! The unused espresso pot shouted: to take up valuable space! The ceiling-mounted surfboard sung with several different-pitched voices in harmony: to keep reminding you of something you will never remember! Five old mobile phones murmured in tandem: hm... to rob you of your... attention? The dreamer on the beanbag looked up at these objects dancing around in a circle in the small living room, dancing so fast that after a while they started to form a shimmering tunnel, which of course was a portal to another scene in the dream, a scene where the dreamer Bjørn could see an older version of himself preparing to feed an Iberian lynx a live rabbit. The rabbit was kicking at his stomach, terrified-eyed, scratching his skin, while the Iberian lynx' claws was tearing at the flesh of his other arm, until this older self became so frustrated it decided to kill both animals. It did this by pressing the 'enter' button on a laptop computer, all the while laughing. Which action naturally introduced a vast sun-scorched plane – a sand-covered stretch littered with sad-looking broken lamp-posts and long-corroding steel beams, despondent heaps of different-coloured bricks, unrecognisable plastic shapes all over the place, sulking, putty and PVC fittings shaped like giant spider-webs, all tangled and crying, broken and broken-hearted advertising screens, enormous smashed-in and tire-less dumpers, all humming together a spaghetti-western version of a lullaby Bjørn had found terribly sad as a child, the words having changed:

Who can bu-ild with-out a heart?
Who can weld with-out oxy-gen?
Who can run with-out oil and gas?
Who can we call for main-ten-ance?

The sun was setting fast at the end of this impossibly vast plane. Bjørn was starting to feel cold in the dream, all the while observing this darkening scene from his supine position on the enormous beanbag, aware of the snow falling outside the window, that someone had come back home, had opened the apartment's front door and was shouting his name. His lucidly dreaming self was trying to wake up, but realising he wouldn't be able to, because he was to blame, just as much as…

His mother laid a hand on his shoulder and Bjørn woke up gasping for air, like he'd come up from deep water, from under layers and layers of something heavy.

"Bjørn?"

He looked at his mother, confused, parts of him still sleeping.

"What?"

"You were screaming."

"Oh…"

"Were you dreaming?"

She looked worried. He could see this even though the room was unlit.

"I think so."

"But you're awake now. I'm here."

"Yes."

He looked to his right, at the snowflakes falling through the darkness.

"What was the dream about?"

His mind drifted off trying to remember the essence of it, the something he could still feel, a deep melancholia it was impossible to describe.

"I don't know," he said. "It just feels sad now. That it was a very sad dream. Filled with lots of… I don't remember."

His mother nodded, as if she'd been having similar dreams lately.

"And how was your day?" she asked. "Greenwich?"

Bjørn shook his head almost invisibly, his eyes watering.

"I think it's over down there," he said. "It's terrible."

"I was afraid so. And the people?"

"I don't know. I really don't know. Where do they go? What can they have left?"

They both looked out the window, as if the snow had answers.

"I don't know either," his mother said whispering. "It's a mystery. They just disappear. Nobody knows where to. With relatives maybe? Down in Brighton? In snow-caves somewhere? Who knows? I asked the Mayor about it today and he just shook his head. I'm not sure he's even listening anymore."

She got up from her knees with a lot of pain and walked over to the wobbly IKEA table where she lit a candle.

"I know," Bjørn said. "Kweku told me earlier he's had problems getting through to him too. He says he fears his magnet has lost its way? Has he told you this theory? It sounded spot on to me. I've never seen him so, so directionless. What do you think we should do?"

"About the Mayor?"

"Yes?"

"I don't know."

She stared at the candle flame.

"Go on I guess. Try to get on top of things. He's mostly been in the way anyway, right from the beginning."

Bjørn could see his mother was exhausted. It was really getting to her. She'd been working non-stop for months already. While the snow had just kept falling and piling up. Whatever she did it didn't really make a difference. And no one was giving her feedback, helping her set goals, pushing her on. He'd tried, but knew he wasn't helping. His suggestions and plans and statistics were too impractical, too removed and theoretical. And still, the terrible fact remained: it was his fault that she was there. Yes. Yes. It was. But. The thought was too devastating to really. He couldn't allow. No. He had to suppress. Otherwise he didn't know what he'd do.

"Why don't you sit down?" he said, scrambling to his feet. "And I'll make us an Irish coffee?"

"That's a good idea," she said, tearing her gaze away from the flame. She smiled at him that smile he remembered so well from his childhood. The one that still made him feel that everything would be all right.

/>

<trivia

Did you know that most schools had not been open for many months? That the younger kids of Tower Hamlets were forgetting what basic learning they might've absorbed? That teachers up and down the borough were getting seriously depressed thinking of this? Of having to teach the same kids the same things again, over and over again, one more time? Did you know that, on average, out of ten volunteers for snow-plough service only two could go straight through to vehicle training, the rest were either sent home or in a few cases not even admitted to the temporary recruiting-offices, which strictly speaking made the two out of ten statistic a bit off? Did you know that most people, when it came down to it, actually wanted to work? That most people found it terrible to sit still and do nothing with the prospect of nothing to do all day, week after week, despite the pre-snow stories in the tabloids about the laziness of people, the couch-potato generation? Did you know that a group of young Somali men in Southwark had been going door-to-door every day for four months asking residents if they needed any help? That a lot of others were following their example? Did you know that the average Internet withdrawal syndrome sufferer dreamt of opening tabs and buying apps well into the fifth month of no Internet access? That he or she would remember their passwords till the day he or she died, contrary to all talk of forgetting passwords and needing computers to help us remember them? Did you know you could ski from Finsbury Park to Peckham in just under twenty minutes with the wind in your back? That it became popular to say 'keys' when referring to a pair of 'skis'? As in, *I've got a new pair of keys yo*? Or, *check out my keys yo, how they glide, man*? Did you know you could make a decent pair of snowshoes by melting together two or more pairs of flip-flops? That most so-called winter shoes sold in London prior to the crisis were absolutely rubbish when it came to keeping you warm and dry? That you'd be better off wrapping and strapping a couple of take-out pizza-cartons around your ankles and filling them with oatmeal? Did you know that seeds were freezing in the ground? Becoming permanently damaged? That the trees' bark was eaten under the cover of snow by mice and rats and ants? Did you know that prisons had started letting prisoners loose? Because they couldn't find enough staff? Because the growing layer of snow was making it inhuman to keep people locked up? People who might not be able to get out without anyone's help? Did you know that the prospect of becoming a father or a mother had stopped appealing to large sections of the population aged between 20 and 35? Did you know that a new ice age was statistically 99.8% likely to happen? Did you know that in all probability you could not have lived a life very different from the one you ended up living? No matter how hard you applied yourself? Did you know that around 63% of the population entertained thoughts of living forever? That they believed that by the time they were old the fountain of youth would've been discovered? Did you also know you could actually die of boredom? That your dreams were probably the most exciting experiences you would ever have? That while sleeping you could therefore be considered more *alive* than when you were awake? Did you know that there was no such thing as giving up? Only giving in?

/>

/art

Started at Sun Sep 17 02:11:59 27020

Command line was: ./henkick_1263 --out-dir=store/
final_rebuild --out-postfix=arx_run_0_no_clean
--creat-sigma=10 --no-plot --save-plot --kwg-
base=hk_kwg_9.db --drives-list=drives.txt --drive-
idx=102

Version tag 3.12.1.1263, built Sun Sep 17 02:11:56
27020

Job ID is: 942994, 1378 instances allocated

VC hash: b6c71af5b2fa

parsing recovered files at /store/recovery/
drvM8C

<the_bleeding_heart

The Dane left the apartment. He took the elevator with the mirrors he never looked directly into. He walked through the lobby lined with trees the management had put in just after the place was built, in the spirit of newness one would guess, trees that were now dead, just left, wilting away, an overt offence to everyone who lived there. He stepped into the foggy evening en route to his girlfriend. The fog made him look up just after leaving the building. He glinted into the sharply dispersed light from a nearby lamp-post. He put his hands inside his coat's well-worn pockets and looked up, the way he'd done as a boy, looking up at a friend's house after he'd thrown a few pebbles at the window.

He thought he smelled snow. He lowered his gaze and stepped forward. He hadn't smelled snow in almost five years.

He walked past Wimpy Burger. He passed the Bleeding Heart. The kind of pub the Dane would've loved to have a drink in, just once, say on a quiet random weekday afternoon, just to be in there, alone with the old Irishmen, and look out on the street, and not in, as he always did. As for the Wimpy Burger, he might've been in there, maybe twice, but he didn't remember exactly. The same was actually true for the Bleeding Heart. He'd been too drunk that night. He thought it didn't count as "having been there" if he couldn't remember.

Deeper parts of him knew now it was going to snow. The fog was so thick and flew by so quickly there was no mistaking the signs if you'd ever lived somewhere it snowed occasionally. The body knew.

This was Shadwell. It was going to snow, and the thought made the Dane happy for a brief moment.

He passed the Library and walked down Watney Market to Commercial Road, head lowered, as usual – walking towards the bus he would take to Bank. The DLR wasn't running. From Bank he needed to take the Northern Line all the way to Hampstead, where Alice lived; his dark-haired, almost mute girlfriend.

It was going to snow. The Dane smelled it. And he was right. The first flakes were forming in the air above Shadwell. Unusually thick rags, crystals the size of crumbled

Kleenex, forming and falling above the East of London, close to the river. As the Dane stepped onto the number 15, the first of these freakishly large snowflakes hit the bus's windscreen, like a piece of soft, almost weightless fudge.

/>

<tutorial

Earlier that same day. The Dane was seated in a deep, almost soggy cushioned chair in the tiny office of his assigned supervisor. The office was at the top of the college's main building and must have been a broom-closet at some point. You could still almost smell the chlorine and the drying, mouldy mops. The Dane's legs were somehow filling the whole room, it felt like, at least from where the Dane was sitting, sinking further and further into the soft chair. He could see the squat, pale-faced, dark-haired supervisor between the twin peaks of his own knees.

This was their first meeting. The supervisor was completely against college regulation smoking a roll-up and the small window was open and a cold draft was hitting the Dane's right side. Did PhD students tend to pass out during tutorials? Was that the reason for the soft, low-to-the-ground chair? There was clearly some kind of power structure and play implied in this seating arrangement.

The tiny supervisor was perched on his swivel chair, his feet dangling freely above the floor. He motioned a little with his hip giving the chair a mini-twist around its axis. Above him, seen from the Dane's deep perspective, were shelves upon shelves of the heaviest art-books, coffee-table tomes, books better used as part of a solid foundation for something big (an outhouse?). It felt like they were going to come crashing down any minute, missing the small supervisor but landing on the Dane, in his lap and groin, on his face and head.

The Dane was hungover. His mind felt three clicks to the left of some personal norm he wouldn't be able to identify or think of when not hungover. Dreamy, detached, apprehensive. It felt like he could reach out and lift the little supervisor and place him on his knee. The supervisor had a very unhealthy aura, the Dane thought, which was a thought he would normally never think.

It was freezing in the little office, surely formerly a broom-closet. The Dane's upper body was positively reclined. He covered his chest with his jacket. The supervisor completed the call and put out the tiny roll-up that hadn't been lit for the last couple of minutes. The

Dane imagined smelling the supervisor's fingers up close and immediately felt nauseous. The room was not lit by anything other than the streak of daylight coming through the small window.

"So Knud..."

The Dane met the supervisor's eyes though they didn't meet his.

"Surname. Let's see... Bonaparte? Is that your real surname?"

"Yes."

"Your mother was a historian?"

"Sorry...?"

"Your mother, she... your name, she was an academic?"

"Oh... No."

It must be depressing working here, the Dane thought. How could he come in here every day? And was that a Taschen book? Helmut Newton?

"Denmark. So does that mean overseas fees?"

"Sorry?"

"Are you registered as an overseas student? You know we take in a lot of overseas students, mostly Japanese girls, to fund this new program?"

"No. I didn't know. Denmark is in the EU."

"So maybe we took you in on some merit then?"

"...?"

"Anyway. I'm your supervisor. My name is Charles."

His voice was really deep for someone so small. Hoarse.

"You're a performance artist it says?"

The Dane's hangover was quickly turning into a minor depression. He sighed and looked out the window that was only showing him grey sky.

"I don't know... I wouldn't call it performance. That's too narrow."

"OK, what are you then?"

"I don't know. I haven't come up with. I don't know. Is it important?"

The supervisor looked incredulously at the Dane. His stare almost nasty.

"Let me tell you a few things about the art world then, Bonaparte, if that's what you want to be called, straight from the outset, so that we'll have no illusions here, as it were, going forward..."

The supervisor's short arms were folded over his small chest, his dark thin hair feebly framing both sides of his face, sticking to the pasty hollow cheeks. His mandatory black turtleneck was almost touching his chin. It must be itchy, the Dane thought.

"This is not a place for idealists, OK? The art world, and trust me on this, is about knowing what you are, and doing it well. And doing it over and over again, consistently, you see... until some day, perhaps someone notices you out of the sheer force of the repetition you've put into the world, OK? So any ideas... let's say, you might have about freely following your ideas and intuitions, and so on... forget them now, immediately, or go home, OK? Is that clear?"

The supervisor tried to swallow to avoid an acid burp. His face went faintly purple.

"If you want to succeed that is. Then, that's what you have to do."

The Dane felt both sad and angry, like laughing and hitting the supervisor, maybe holding him and shaking him head-down over his desk, bumping his head against the ashtray, then punching him in his miniature nuts.

"Trust me, I've seen people like you come in here and sticking to their idealistic guns and never coming to see me again for another tutorial. And after they're done here they go home to where they crawled out from. From somewhere under a rock in northern Europe, or Japan, perhaps a cave, and take up bar-tending. Trust me on this Bonaparte, trust me... I've seen it happen again and again and again and again."

The supervisor reached for a crumbled bag of Drum roll-up tobacco and started rolling a very thin one. Tobacco-threads were falling in his lap and on the desk. He put a little white filter in one end and tapped the cigarette on his Bic.

The Dane was lying on his back in the low chair by now, still covered by his jacket. He felt like getting up and leaving but not without first having done some serious physical and mental harm to this tiny prick on the swivel chair.

"It says here that you act, take photographs. Make films...?"

"Yes."

"So which is it?"

"What do you mean?"

"Do you want to act, be a photographer, or make films? Which is it?"

The Dane raised himself up so his head was level with the supervisor's groin.

"None of those things."

"None?"

"Yes. None."

"So what are we doing here then? This isn't for pissing around, a post-graduate art degree."

The Dane didn't fully understand the expression *pissing around*, but felt really angered by it anyway, maybe too much. Should he just leave? Slap him? He sat up as much as physically possible in the low and soft chair.

"Listen Knud... I can see that you're ticked off and that's fine. That's why I'm telling you this. You *should* be ticked off. I just want you to think really really hard about what you want to do. I've seen it all and it's not pretty. Trust me. People go literally insane here. Get hospitalised. Become alcoholics..."

The supervisor lit the thin roll-up and inhaled an amount of smoke that didn't even come out again when he started talking.

"What you've done so far was just that. Just what you've done so far. Now. Now starts the tough part, OK? What are you going to do from now on? That's the question. What are you interested in? And I mean *really really* interested in?"

His double emphasis of the word went into a slight falsetto. The Dane lifted and lowered his eyebrows a few times while looking absentmindedly at his knees in the black denims.

"You have to focus. You see, you can't afford to dilly dally around. Trust me. This is tougher than, than... investment banking. These are like, I don't know, preparations for the Mental Olympics or something. You see what I mean?"

Different new thoughts were appearing from out of nowhere and swam around in the Dane's mind like scavenger-fish around a dying whale, the dying or dead whale being partly his sense of purpose and self, partly old emotions and old thoughts connected to his sense of purpose and self, its concepts and notions and...

He felt a sweet and sour anticipatory cramp somewhere in his lower abdomen. A mixture of the supervisor's words and the tobacco smoke in the room had made him urgently need the bathroom.

/>

<tourist_racist

From inside the bus the Dane couldn't see the snow falling while the windows were covered with steam. Too many passengers had been breathing in and out for too long already. The windows were shut and he couldn't reach one to open it. The thought of the stagnant air repulsed him. He tried to focus on something else, but it was hard – it was there, so fucking present, so in his face, in his mouth, in his nose. The bus was a symbol of nearly all the things he hated about London. The human mass squeezed into it and asked to bunch up and fight for a place to rest a leg or an arm, or God forbid, a bag or a suitcase.

It made him angry. Why did it have to be this way? Why did they have to settle for this? What did it take to transport people a few miles in dignity? Come on! He wanted someone to answer these questions.

The free newspapers left everywhere littered the floor along with the half-drunk cans of Irn-Bru or Lucozade that had toppled over and now rolled back and forth as the bus turned, little by little emptying their sugary leftovers onto the floor until it formed a Pollockian pattern sticky as fly-paper. He had reluctantly pulled himself to the upper deck and even more reluctantly found a seat toward the back. Now he sat there with one arse-cheek just about touching down, as non-committal as possible to the whole concept of "taking the bus".

On the seat inside him sat a girl, maybe thirteen, of West-Indian heritage, listening to music from an mp3 player of unknown brand and quality, blasting it out from the loosely worn headphones, irritating the Dane. He thought the rhythm of the music could be mistaken for any rhythm from any number of R&B songs produced in any year, going back maybe six or seven years. The whole thing sounded awful, tinny and forced to the Dane.

He'd actually enjoyed taking the bus on rare occasions before, as an ethnographer perhaps enjoys being with a new tribe for the first couple of months. He'd been able to sit back and think of it as an absurdist play with no plot and meaning, other than the inherent meaning and plot all things had, at a basic level. The bus had been less crowded and the windows without steam then, allowing a touristy perspective on the city. With his head full of art theory he'd seen himself as some sort of documentarian of "life lead by normal people". He'd enjoyed that, that point of view, that pulled-back perspective, even to the point of thinking about it as a potential part of his next installation.

Was he being racist when he actually accepted the fact that he didn't like R&B?

What was a definition of a racist anyway?

Was he one because he didn't like where he lived? Next to a Bangladeshi family of six whose cooking he could always smell and whose laundry he always saw hanging over the railing in the common area of the apartment building? Did that constitute bigotry? Just not liking it? Not being familiar with it and frankly not finding it all that great and inspiring? Was that racism? Wishing he could live in a better neighbourhood? Wishing he had the money to rent an apartment somewhere nice and convenient, where most people would look and behave like he did? Was that racism?

He found it unbearable to be nice just because if you weren't nice you were an arsehole bigot. Why weren't Chinese tourists detested more? Why were the fucking

Aussies and Kiwis, running around from bar to pub to bar in their shorts, flip-flops and rugby shirts, accepted? Tolerated?

What was the difference? Why differentiate? This bad conscience towards the dark and yellow-skinned, all because of a measly few hundred years of pillaging and raping the world? When could that be done with?

Did he just not like people? Was that his problem?

He often felt this way. But then again, the young girl sitting next to him. A person from a background so remote from his. What about *her*? He almost felt compelled to ask her what it had been like. Growing up the way she'd done.

So he had that, a strong curiosity; he felt it redeemed him some.

Because: he was nearly as good at self-reproach as he was at disliking things around him. He was aware of this. He was aware of his almost debilitating self-awareness. He knew he was a crank. Knew that everyone scrambled for a living. Most people working their arses off to pay the rent, while he walked around idle, doing nothing, for weeks. Six months in London and he was already fed up with its daily avalanche of contradictions. He often wished he'd never come. He couldn't have foreseen the sheer intensity of it: the numbing display of hopelessness, the terrible traffic, the shitty housing, the loneliness.

/>

<no_messages_no_news

The Dane's girlfriend Alice wore black at all times, teenage-black, in perpetual opposition to everything, absolutely everything. Her hair was dyed black, her trousers were black, her sweaters were black, her shoes were black, her make-up was black. She was not ready for love and a stable relationship, but she had the quality of caring, which made her care too much of course – this quality of caring being the direct source of her state of near clinical anxiety for the *what* and the *why* and the *where* about the Dane that night.

He'd said he'd be at hers by 11 p.m. at the latest, and by 1 a.m. he still hadn't shown up. She'd been watching the BBC's special newscast about the bad weather until the TV had gone dark around 11.45 p.m. Tube-trains were apparently stuck underground due to a power failure presumably caused by too many homeowners simultaneously turning on electrical heaters. The surge had knocked out both the Northern Line's main and back-up supply. The Dane could theoretically be anywhere under the ground then, or maybe at home, or somewhere else. His phone went straight to his provider's standard message for when it was either out of power, out of credit, or simply had been neglected for too long, which was not the most confidence-inducing message when her anxiety level was already filling her stomach with that horrible feeling of not knowing.

<watching_tv_growing_up

Growing up in rural Denmark there wasn't much to do apart from watching TV. The Dane lived with his only sister, five years older, his mother, and her ever-changing flux of partners. These men would sometimes beat her. He would listen to it lying in bed. His room was at the top of the house with a view of the apple orchard and the field beyond. From begging his mother, and because she felt guilty for dragging these violent men into the house, she'd bought him a TV to keep in his room. It stood next to the window with the view of the apple orchard and the field. His mother had met his father once and as a result he'd been born. His sister left home when she was sixteen and would only visit when he begged her to. She came twice a year maybe and would take him to the local seaside town, together with her boyfriend, always the same one. He became good friends with his sister's boyfriend, who taught him how to shoot at beer-bottles with a rifle from a distance. His sister and the boyfriend would lie on a blanket behind him, kissing and speaking quietly. He would turn to look at them in between shots and they wouldn't notice, or at least they would pretend he wasn't looking, which he liked. It felt good just being near them and shooting at the empty beer bottles.

But mostly he'd spent his evenings in his single bed watching cable-TV. His room faced north so the sun never shone directly into it and therefore he could keep the blinds up, leaving the treetops exposed and the changing evening sky always just a glance away from the TV. The light in the sky would go from a warm afternoon glow through a pinkish sunset into a grey blue twilight. Sometimes the sunrays would shine onto dark rain-clouds and in summer lightning and thunder quite frequently erupted from those dark clouds, so loudly that he had to turn the volume up. The rain fell heavily then, and washed down the large single windowpane. He would pull the duvet under his chin, wearing his clothes still. He was already quite tall and had to bend his knees to keep his feet covered. He watched American sitcoms and drama series like Alf and Married With Children and The Wonder Years and 90210

and MacGyver and Baywatch and A-Team and Airwolf, and
a bit later MTV's first Real World and The Simpsons, but
he didn't really like or get The Simpsons until he was older.

On Tuesdays the line-up of shows was such that he
didn't have to leave the room or switch channel, but could
stay in bed and watch all evening until about midnight
when he eventually got undressed and closed the blinds.
His mother would fetch him snacks and food, always feeling
so guilty for bringing home the violent drunken men, and
for not really knowing how to raise a son and take care
of him and talk to him and show him the affection she
really had for him.

When the fighting and hitting and screaming started,
the young Dane would simply turn up the volume, quietly
tip-toe over to the door, and turn the key, worried about
his mother and wondering if there was anything he could
do, though there was nothing, short of calling the police,
but he didn't want to do that, fearing they would put
him in a foster home and make his mother's life even
more miserable.

He fantasised about Winnie Cooper from The Wonder
Years, and as soon as he was able to, and understood how
to, he masturbated whenever she was on screen, making
sure he let go of his member whenever that little annoying
kid narrator showed his face. When the Wonder Years was

over and 90210 came on he made sure he had a t-shirt or a sock at hand so he could keep tugging at his junior whenever Brenda or Kelly or Donna (particularly Donna) came on screen. Again, he would let go when Brandon or Steve or Dylan appeared, but if they were in the same scene, as they often annoyingly were, he sometimes just had to concentrate on Donna and imagine her in his blue painted room with the view across the orchard and the field beyond, how she would lay down beside him and kiss him softly and how he would fall asleep in her arms. That was what he most often fantasised about: falling asleep, held by Donna, confused about the mechanics of sex and whatever it was that men and women did when they were in bed together. He ejaculated fantasising about sleeping in Donna's arms, the swallows outside his window coming home for the night, and thankfully sometimes his mother's boyfriend didn't hit her and he'd fall asleep without being afraid and worried.

Sports on TV was another friend. It didn't really matter what sport it was, as long as it was considered sports. With the introduction of the Eurosport channel the young Dane had access to round-the-clock action. If there was no good sitcom on, or drama, he watched football from all the European leagues, handball, curling, ice hockey, alpine skiing, cross-country skiing, darts, gymnastics, cycling, rowing and every other televised sport imaginable. He knew the scores and table positions of five or six different sports across the whole of continental Europe. He watched delayed emissions, hoping the event organisers would get hold of a wind-machine to blow the weather the hell away so he could see the men hurl themselves expertly down the mountainsides of Austria or Switzerland or France, and sometimes Aspen and Vail, Colorado.

He would feel a deep connection with the TV on days like that, connected to the drama of winning and losing, rooting for his favourite skiers and hitting the wall with his flat hand if a despised Austrian won with only a slight margin. The hand burned afterwards and he would be shocked at how engaged he'd become. A sudden hollow feeling came over him and he would stare out the window over the apple orchard and the field beyond and hope his mother wouldn't bring home another unknown man that night, and the clarity of the light and the way it shone on the treetops and the clouds etched into him a complete image of loneliness.

The worst was whenever a storm or repair-works cut off TV access for a period of time. He lay in bed listening to the sounds of the house, suddenly so present and terrifying, reminding him of where he was and what was going on right there. The ticking of the large clock in the living room could be heard through the floor, the wind catching the wall and rustling the leaves of the apple trees, water forever running in the toilet due to a leaking gasket, the static from the TV's loudspeakers, the neighbour's car coming back from town, a tractor ploughing a field in the distance. He saw the swallows come and leave their nest underneath the roof, completely silent in their flight, but making a barely audible scratching sound as they folded their wings and rubbed them against the wooden wall when feeding their young. Further away he saw crows and seagulls fly, sometimes geese in formation. The blue of his room faded into a darkness whenever he was looking out the window during the day. He pulled the duvet up under his chin and warmed his hands between his thighs.

When the TV finally came back to life he relaxed again. And if the day was right and the time was early evening, Donna might be on, or Winnie Cooper shyly smiling at him, and for a few hours he would be with his friends in America, connected and gone, escaped into somewhere nice.

/>

<a_boat_at_sea

So the Dane was a boat at sea belonging nowhere, his appointed therapist had said, and a boat at sea looking for a female harbour, the therapist had maintained, floating willy-nilly, was not a boat ready for love and steadiness in a female harbour. No, the boat at sea needed to build its own harbour first, so that the female harbour could think of the boat's visit as a checking-out visit, not a desperately-lonely-sacking-of-the-female-harbour's-emotional-defences visit. The female harbour needed to know that the male visiting boat was just a casual browser who would return home to its own moorings and perhaps someday in a calm and pleasant future send a convoy asking for the harbour's permission to perhaps consider the male boat's next arrival as perhaps something a little more intimate, maybe even a date.

The Dane was definitely not a male boat with the type of time, leisure and means that would allow for such courtship of female harbours. His way, when he'd had it, had been to go up to Alice, two bottles of wine on his way to the ocean floor, asking if she wouldn't mind buying him another, he was out of money – that she could join him for a glass, she looked miserable too. To which piece of naval gallantry Alice had been unable to muster anything but a weak hoisting of her neutrality flag and had put the money in his hand.

They had become boyfriend and girlfriend that night.

But the male boat drifting at sea, how could it build a harbour? How could the rudderless anxious self-conscious male boat ever get to land, and find the materials to build a harbour that would, in time, afford him the qualities of stability and dependability? And what if this boat afloat at sea had no interest in building a harbour? But still wanted love? Still wanted to be able to share parts of his life with a woman? What then?

One should think that a boat was made to be at sea, and not in a harbour. But the harbourless boat was suspicious. The harbourless man was dangerous. He stood there in the living room of a well-educated girl's apartment and oozed destruction – spelled E.N.T.R.O.P.Y.

Since the Dane had left Denmark, since he'd literally

dropped out of university five years earlier, since he'd realised he didn't belong in Denmark, since he'd realised he didn't belong in London either, since his mother had died, since his sister had stopped talking to him, since he was a young boy, since he became aware that the life people around him were living was not for him, that he couldn't live it, or lie it (as he used to say), since many other things, he had not wanted to build a harbour, secretly knowing this all along, knowing he would be incapable of it, knowing he didn't want to spend his life doing it, feeling that, every time he even considered starting something 'proper', he wilted away very visibly to himself, within.

Though Alice was his port of call on lonely nights, but never for more than two nights in a row. She felt more like a fellow vagabond, like a co-bum cut loose from the rhythms of normal life, shacking up in Pirate Bay together with him, many miles away from any tax-funded, government-regulated, publically cleaned and maintained facilities.

He'd stood in a few normal girls' rooms, for a moment enthralled by a fantasy of belonging, looking at the spines of the large books on the shelves, smelling the fresh flowers present in such rooms, and had always felt a profound urge to lie down on the sofa and sleep, fully dressed, with his shoes on. It had felt to the Dane in such moments that he was surely the figment of someone's imagination; that he would have liked to escape that imagination, to escape the book, the play or film about him.

Being in a girl's house, in her room, in her parent's living room, in her dad's study, he'd always felt at the point of breaking out of the narrative, so that, if he'd been able to open the door to the patio, he could've run clear from his `[syntax error]`

`/>`

Copenhagen, 23.09.17

Dear Knud Nielsen,

Regarding your application for funding from the Danish Arts Council for the project entitled "Promises to Keep"

We regret to inform you that we are unable at present to support your proposed project while we find that its general un-Danish character and intended audience lies outside of what the Danish Arts Council regards as its mandate to support.

Should you wish to reconsider some of the parameters of your project, in particular to move it from the UK and give it a more Danish context, we should be happy to process your funding application once more.

We wish you all the best in finding support for your project, which we found an intriguing and exciting read.

With sincere regards,

Nora Rasmussen

Secretary to the Funding Committee

Danish Arts Council

/>

<comparative_literature

The Dane had started studying comparative literature at the University of Aarhus, with no real plan for what to do with it. He'd discovered while he was still in school that he was a good reader, meaning, he understood something about books, how they were connected, one book to another, across the span of time and geography, referring to each other, building and expanding on each other's themes. He could talk about his experience of books in a way that made others listen. Maybe he read difficult books due to his mother's absolute disdain for anything other than crime fiction. By the age of fifteen he'd stopped talking to her though they still lived in the same house. She wasn't able to talk much by then anyway, her alcohol consumption chaining her to the couch for most of the day, nursing what sounded like violent hangovers. Difficult novels provided not only escape but a feeling of seriousness, a feeling that life might be liveable on different terms.

Cases like the Dane's usually had two outcomes. The first and most chosen: delinquency, correction and abuse (self and others). The second: a struggle for betterment, a constant combat against one's own past, to be free from it, to not be defined by one's parents. He chose the latter, or to speak of choice might be facetious, but at least he didn't become a stereotypical victim of a difficult childhood, banging up cars, breaking and entering, fighting other hoodlums, mostly because he didn't want to be what she was. For all he could think of was to be different from her. He even ditched the TV (she watched a lot of it when she was getting drunk). He'd had his fill anyway.

No, it was books, difficult books. At university he developed the identity that came with reading serious books: he became an intellectual – at war with the normality of life, at war with its banality, at war with big emotions and girls and cars and the triviality of newspapers and the meaninglessness of chitchat. He became an aspiring artist. He went to university to read books and had no plan for what to do with his degree once he was forced to leave the institution. His correction had not been administered by the state. He had chosen his own regime. But as prison drops you on its doorstep with no real capacity to re-integrate, so the university, particularly the faculties of the humanities, spits you out after five or six years of hard labour, just as incapable of making your way into a good life.

He wrote his thesis on the emergent forms of modern self-identity as evidenced in Don Quixote and Hamlet Prince of Denmark, with a particular emphasis on their confused reflexivity. It was an ambitious project, attempted by many of the field's greatest before him, and his tutors, that is, his only tutor for five years, told him that it might be an idea to find a less obvious and less high-profile project, so as not to be judged against the best works of comparative literary theory, and run the risk of failing, or most likely ending up with something very mediocre. But the Dane was adamant. It was this or nothing. He wanted to tackle the most obvious and the most difficult at the same time. He developed a pathological sense of being both Hamlet and Don Quixote. To study these two men of literature was an opportunity to study himself, his own soul. He felt just like Hamlet in his confused love and hatred of his mother. Just like Don Quixote in his wish to ride into the world and change it. Wasn't he a perfect mix of the two? Well-read, confused, ambitious, handsome, lanky, with a yearning for the meaning of life?

The Dane, owing to his economically deprived family background, had taken advantage of the state's student loan scheme to finance his studies, which was something almost all Danish students did unless they had a rich family, or had an old-school work ethic hammered into them by old-fashioned parents insisting on menial jobs to fund the studying. The student loan scheme was generous. A student could easily study at leisure for a period of six years without thinking about money. Like the Dane did. He didn't think about it one bit. When the end of the sixth year came, and support ran dry, he was still not done with his thesis. And by this time he'd become so accustomed to the idea of not working, as well as thinking of himself as more of an artist than an academic, that the very thought of getting paid work repelled him so much he would rather starve than be humiliated like that, like most people were.

In his Don Quixote fantasies he simply stopped eating, and like Hamlet he started drifting into the middle space between morbid angst and lack of resolve. In his mostly unfurnished apartment close to campus he lay down on his bed feeling faint. His bedclothes were unchanged for two months and were stiff as papyrus from sweat. His duvet smelled sweetly like medicine taken by people who suffered unusual digestive diseases. The amount of time he could work with a modicum of intelligent alertness dwindled every week, until after nearly three months of starvation and isolation he finally collapsed as he went outside on a rare occasion to get another book from the library. The owner of a local pub found him on the pavement outside the sports equipment shop on Nørrebrogade. The elderly man said he'd never seen anyone so thin since the day the papers carried photos of Auschwitz survivors. The Dane was sent to hospital and never went back to that University, his thesis still unfinished, a comprehensive mess of notes and drafts and redrafts.

/>

<alice_couldnt_take_it

The Dane's girlfriend Alice couldn't really take waiting for him anymore. She sat in the windowsill of her studio apartment in Hampstead, close to the Heath (then already covered in a thick layer of the freshly falling snow). It was probably not far enough down to kill her unless she jumped headfirst, which thought was too gruesome to really take seriously. The snow might even cushion the fall if she decided to go at it that way. And then what? She'd be a basket case? Ah non, pas ça! But she couldn't take sitting still anymore either, so what would give? Some temporary remedy? The only alcohol she had in the house was a bottle of Grand Marnier. The cigarettes were almost out. But she had to do something. She couldn't just sit there anymore. Waiting for him. Not knowing. So she poured a glass of the liquor, sipped it, grinned and smoked two cigarettes lighting one with the other. Then there were no more cigarettes. And she couldn't really drink without smoking. But she'd started and didn't want to stop, feeling increasingly desperate for another cigarette.

So then what?

She chugged a full glass of Grand Marnier and almost puked it straight up, coughing violently. She stood in the middle of her room: books, papers, clothes, magazines, dirty plates on the floor around her, tears coming down her pale cheeks. Another full glass then. This time less of a problem. She felt the coming on of the fuzzy edges. Another glass. She downed it. That tasted OK. She smiled. Then she laughed a high-pitched laugh and took a large swig from the bottle, which made her cough again. Coughing done she went dead serious, standing completely still in the middle of her cluttered room, sensing an inner rotation she was sure she'd never felt before. Then she laughed again, manically, and felt superfuzzy, not only at the edges. She stepped over to the wall and beat her head hard against it, twice. Tiny sparks appeared and disappeared in the circumference of her vision, miniature galaxies born and dying at a rapid clip. She lay down and started crying, silently first, then gasping for air, her whole body shaking. Then she moaned loudly as she managed to breathe again and continued crying.

Outside her small window the snowflakes floated slowly to the ground. The night was eerily quiet. No alarms were heard, no sirens. No cars were driving on the road. The shadow of a lone person was moving, bent forward, northwards; then was gone. A family of deer emerged from a thicket at the edge of the park. Their heads motioning slowly side-to-side, their ears flapping to remove the settling snow. Then they disappeared into the whiteout; ran back into the park again. The snow kept falling. It landed thick on the power line extending from wooden pole to wooden pole down the road. There was no wind. The flakes swirled uninterrupted according to the aerodynamics of their individual shapes. A snow-covered fox crossed the road. Within a few minutes its tracks were completely gone.

>

<the_sky_was_breathing

It felt like the sky was breathing. The further the Dane walked from the shop where he'd bought and finished the bottle of vodka, and the more sober he got, the less he was able to shake the feeling that the sky was breathing, that the sky's breath's vapour was turning into snowflakes. He didn't know where he was, where he was walking, though he observed he was walking in the opposite direction of most people. Almost everyone came huddling towards him, alone, fast-paced, their heads bent forward and down, full of purpose. He walked slowly towards them with his head high and the snowflakes settling in his hair, on his forehead and eyebrows. The strangers bumped into him and rushed on without apologising.

The snow on the ground lay a good thirty centimetres

deep. It had been snowing for five hours solid – since he boarded the bus in Shadwell earlier that evening.

He'd come up from the tube at Belsize Park. His face was partly smudged from having touched the tunnel wall with his hand and then having touched his face (as he'd made his way from the stalled train). He was too agitated to remember why he was out walking – to pay any real attention to where he was. The bottle of vodka had not helped; mostly it had delayed and complicated his emotions. He had a woolly feeling he was somehow responsible for something he couldn't remember. He realised he was cold, that his feet were wet, that his clothes were summer-clothes. Most people kept walking towards him. The experience in the stalled and darkened tube-train had been so overwhelming that his mind had suppressed it for him, for a while. In the darkness, among the screams and banging on the train's windows, his brain had somehow extended a protective bubble for his claustrophobia, lending him a space to act in.

Gradually sobering up from a litre of vodka was hard work. He felt his peripheral vision returning, but with it he felt essential oils evaporating from his muscles and intest-ines, leaving a grimy residue that coated everything inside.

Groping for the emergency exit he'd walked across people's backs and arms. He'd pushed people onto the floor.

He felt like the sky was breathing, that he could breathe with it, that the snowflakes were released from high above with every exhale. He closed his eyes and tilted his head back and felt he was pulling the crystals onto his face when he inhaled.

After a while he opened his eyes and recognised where he was. To his right stood the two giant Egyptian cats guarding the entrance to the old Carreras Cigarette Factory (aka the Arcadia Works and Greater London House). The falling snow piling up had given them both a white beret and was hiding their front paws and seated hind parts. The snow had also given the enormous animals an appearance of being more comfortable, more at home.

Somewhat aware of himself again, of where he was, the Dane started making sense of the stream of people moving towards him. He'd been moving south he realised, although Alice's place lay at the Golders Green side of the Heath, direction north. He realised people had been walking home for hours – that he'd been walking away, at least from where Alice lived.

He checked his pockets for his phone but couldn't find it. He felt for his money, but had none; someone must have stolen it. His keys were gone. He looked at his wrist and saw that he'd lost his watch. He closed his eyes again and took a deep breath. He was sure the sky above him was breathing; that through this activity it was turning itself to snow. He felt brittle and sad and cold. He thought about the worry he was causing Alice. He tried not to think about what he'd expected in the darkness underground.

It felt to the Dane like he'd been given another chance, another ticket to the fair, randomly, undeservedly. And what was he going to do with it? Was he going to try to steal another bottle of vodka, as he wanted to, or was he going to sit this one out and see what might happen at the other end of the hangover?

He opened his eyes. London was starting to disappear. Wet sleet was clinging to the large abandoned tower blocks of the Ampthill council estate, to his left. The yellow streetlight from Hampstead Road didn't reach far beyond the barbed wire fence surrounding the imposing structures. The towers seemed to be growing taller and whiter by the minute, as if they'd given up on the city, listening to a different idea of development.

The Dane felt sad he couldn't be with Alice, that he couldn't tell her where he was. She wasn't perhaps the one he'd hoped to spend his life with, and he admitted he hadn't really looked forward to seeing her that evening, but he knew she would be worried, that she wasn't good at dealing with worry, that she'd treated him much better than he'd ever treated her. He thought that love was perhaps more a question of companionship, when it came down to it, that it had to do with accepting your place and trajectory; that to make it work you had to stop trying to get to somewhere else all the time.

But how could they do that when he knew they were deeply unhappy where they lived? When their options where dwindling the older they got, at least his? As more and more people came to London, from all over Europe, hopeful, looking for a job and an apartment? To make it in the art world?

Perhaps he could find a shop and ask to call Alice from there? Feeling his pockets for his lost phone again he remembered he didn't know her mobile number. And walking further down the street, towards Euston, he noticed that everything had closed up for the night. What time was it? He tried to stop someone walking past him but his arm was brushed away. He tried to ask someone the time and was told to fuck off.

The strangers coming his way, with snow in their hair, walking home, wanted nothing to do with him. His smudged face, his half-drunken babbling and flimsy clothes spelled 'stay away'. Each one avoiding him had seen him being avoided by the person ahead. As he staggered down the pavement, slipping and wildly catching his balance, people started crossing the street to not have to deal with him. He grabbed on to a woman's coat as she tried to flee and she screamed and hit him on the head with her bag and ran away. The spin his body took from losing his grip on her coat made him slip and fall and he rolled onto the pavement, close by the entrance to Euston station.

The sky was most definitely breathing. He felt it, lying on his back in the snow. He felt pressure and release as each breath came down from the clouds and dispersed the snowflakes. He wondered if the blood pumping into his arms and hands was keeping time with the sky's breath. It felt that way, like a giant standing wave (amplitude the height of the atmosphere) was moving up and down, keeping things in time. He smiled and extended his arms. The falling snowflakes melted in his palms. The deepening snow held him comfortably in place. His head felt well supported. The snow muffled the footsteps of the strangers hurrying by. He decided he should only rest for a bit, that he still had things he wanted to do. He would try to get hold of Alice as soon as possible, to figure out a way for them to stay together. He felt ready to let go of things that had made him miserable, his unhappy childhood first of all, his artistic ambitions too. What did he need them for anyway? He was never going to make it – didn't even want to make it anymore, if it was going to be market-led. He would call his sister and suggest they should meet sometime soon, back home in Denmark, where they'd gone Sundays when he was a boy; he could get the ticket on his credit card (he'd find a job to pay it down). He'd never met his nephews. It was about time he did. He decided to cut down on his drinking. Maybe quit outright. He knew that his drinking made him depressed, that he was shortening his years of potentially good health by going at it both hands. Maybe it was time to deal with it? It felt that way, lying there in the snow. It felt like a feasible project. He could at least try. He didn't want to end up like his mother. He knew he had to get away from London, that he had wasted enough time there. He felt very happy making all these plans. He would set things straight – start again. He felt himself growing sleepy. He drifted into sleep.

Then he woke, freezing cold, almost immediately, and opened his eyes with a terrible feeling of having given in – that he'd let go of everything he'd ever held dear. That it would be gone. That his life would not be worth living if he could not have another drink again. That, if he was to spend his life with Alice from that day on, he knew he couldn't find the enthusiasm for it – for the certainty of it, for knowing already at age thirty-eight what his life would be like from that day on, till the moment he died – that there would be no surprises, no more unknown unknowns in such a life. No fun anymore. That there would be no more adventure or randomly following his will. His impulses.

With clarity and a lot of sadness he knew that his project of reform was pure imagination, that he could never do it. Never stick to it. He pushed himself up from the snow and lost his balance and fell over again, but got on his feet and found some support leaning against a lamp-post. There was no doubt the sky was breathing. Snowflakes came floating down in their millions, in an unending exhale from the great mouth above. The houses and streets and traffic lights were shedding skin. The new coat was beautiful. It was thick and white and growing thicker.

/>

/more_snow

Started at Mon Sep 18 04:36:19 27020

Command line was: ./henkick_1264 --out-dir=store/
final_rebuild --out-postfix=arx_run_0_no_clean
--creat-sigma=10 --no-plot --save-plot --kwg-
base=hk_kwg_9.db --drives-list=drives.txt --drive-
idx=103

Version tag 3.12.1.1264, built Mon Sep 18
04:36:16 27020

Job ID is: 361829, 1048 instances allocated

VC hash: 8a5f78b52dc9

parsing recovered files at /store/recovery/drvQ3X

<animal_adventure

Bjørn cut down Clerkenwell Road in a flurry of snow-smoke, the dogs enjoying the pace, then hung an almost sled-toppling right into Southampton Row, where things went a bit slower behind a dumper and a plough clearing a path up to Russell Square. The signal-lights circled into the heavy snowdrift. The dogs grew restless. He tried to calm them but it was hard under the roar of the engines.

After thirty minutes, in deep difficult tracks, Regent's Park lay open and inviting before him. The sound of the dogs was comforting, the ten of them drawing air, their small yelps now and then like children enjoying a favourite dish. They seemed to appreciate the sound of the whip too. Though when it actually hit them they barked, clearly offended.

The park's trees were so completely covered with snow they'd started to resemble rock-formations. Like something transported out of Utah or Idaho, or thereabouts. They gave Bjørn an intense feeling of the far away, of possibilities once glimpsed, something he'd forgotten he'd been into, as a kid, a teenager.

For the first time in a long while he felt the coming on of a smile. He remembered what it had been like to want something. To dream of something. Of somewhere he'd never been perhaps, something he could do at a later stage, when he'd eventually be old enough. To see the world?

But as soon as the smile appeared it went away again, as the sled had pulled to a halt inside the zoo's southern tip, and he looked around.

The scene was appalling. There were large steaming piles of animal excrement all over the place. The vegetation was cut down wherever possible in order to feed some of the hardier animals, the remaining wood hauled inside to stoke the makeshift ovens. The Animal Adventure section had been turned into an animal crematory, with walls of snow packed high around to keep the stench of the burning carcases from the rest of the zoo. The Aardvarks, Porcupines, Sheep, Pigs, Alpacas and Llamas had been relocated to the Outback where they were currently freezing their teats off, in provisory thatch-huts, along with the Wallabies and Emus. So cramped, they were remarkably quiet, waiting, sticking to their species group, shivering, looking wearily around, dozing off, dropping compact strawy turds now and then, urinating as if they weren't aware of doing so.

After snapping a few pictures Bjørn found the B.U.G.S. House and entered the broken door. Inside the mostly dark building it was hard to know what was what. Gradually though, the contours of the display-tanks took shape, and for a while the red, low frequency light sources favoured by insects stood out in the darkness, like distant stars receding through the corridors.

Bjørn looked at his note and knocked on the door with Dr. Balto written on it.

"Come in."

A bright desk lamp dazed him as the door swung open.

"Welcome," said the man sitting in front of the white light.

Bjørn entered and saw that the man's nose had blown up to obscure his left-eye vision, probably due to some insect bite. It was hard to maintain eye contact with him.

"Thanks for coming. In these current conditions..."

Dr. Balto's voice faded as he tilted his head towards a poster of a large hairy spider. There was a faint smell in the room from the animal carcasses over in Animal Adventure.

"It's not so strange, perhaps, in times like these, if people like me are forgotten, do you think? The animal kingdom too?"

The doctor leant back in his chair, crossed his arms over his chest.

"How's that?"

"I don't know. Just look at the ants behind you."

Bjørn leapt forward spastically when he realised the infinite minute movements of the ants kept in the glass-container he'd been leaning up against. The Doctor remained expressionless.

"Who in their right mind would care?"

He proceeded to scratch his bulbous nose delicately with a sharpened pencil. It looked very sore.

"I'm tired I guess. I've been here... feels like almost forever."

Bjørn scratched his own nose in an involuntary reflex. The Doctor sat still, carefully attending to his proboscis with the pencil, giving it a metallic hue in the process, not seeming to focus on anything in particular.

"It's human to do the things humans do I guess. People have to look out for themselves."

The Doctor let his head fall towards the poster of the spider again, putting the pencil down with slow precision.

"How can I help?" Bjørn asked.

He felt sorry for the man. His attempt to keep up some kind of conversation was heartbreaking.

"We need stocktaking."

"OK. How does that work?"

The Doctor picked up the pencil from his cluttered desk again and with a distracted mien started to carefully pass it across the skin of his ballooning inflamed nose, turning towards the spider poster. It was almost as if he was enjoying the sensation, had become addicted to it, to passing the sharp pencil across the scabbing bite-wound, if that was what it was. He turned slowly towards Bjørn again.

"You have to count the animals."

/>

<stocktaking

Bjørn trudged out through the snow-imposed darkness of the B.U.G.S. House into an unmistakable blue hour. The snow looked like it was falling slower than earlier, which was something. But to compensate each snowflake seemed wider and denser than before. Bjørn couldn't remember if it had ever been this cold and still snowing, when he lived in Norway, as a boy, spending most of his time outdoors. Snow usually fell at two to three degrees minus, but this was definitely more like fifteen below. The squeaky sound his boots made was a good indication; nose-hairs stiffening on first inhale too.

He stopped by the Sumatran tiger first. The animal stood on its hind legs, facing away, leaning up against a billboard with the letters SOS written on it. Damp was rising from its mouth with each breath. It was licking snowflakes from the apex of the O. Then it let itself fall down and turned, its giant head directed at Bjørn. It was hard to know through the snowfall and the thick Perspex pane if it had noticed him. Whether it would make any difference to how it behaved.

The tiger came slowly towards him through the blueness of the premature evening, now and then shaking its massive head to get rid of the snow that was quickly settling on it. It walked sullenly, Bjørn thought, like it had been lost in thought for too long, or felt sad about something it had just remembered, something from its childhood, a good experience gone forever perhaps, somewhere in the Sumatran rainforest.

Bjørn got out his clipboard, crunched over to avoid the paper getting wet and noted: Sumatran tiger: I. Then he made sure there were no more of its kind in that enclosure and walked off towards the lions.

Daylight was slipping fast. He estimated he had another half an hour. He bent forward to consult the map just to be sure he wouldn't miss the lions. He figured he was almost there. He stuck the clipboard under his eiderdown jacket and looked around. He'd never been alone in a zoo before. Never been to a zoo in winter before. Branches covered in heavy ice hung dangerously low, about to snap. He had to be careful.

There was a sound of birds in the air. He couldn't tell from where, whether they were crows, seagulls or something more exotic. The smell from the burning carcasses over in Animal Adventure was nauseating. It mixed with the thick fog of stink from all the dung-heaps and yellow patches of urine scattered about. He felt it irritating his throat. Stinging his eyes. The zoo's landscape was confusing. Many of the structures had recently collapsed under the weight of the snow. He realised there was a real possibility that some of the animals were not properly fenced in. It made him feel as though he was being watched. He turned around every few metres to make sure nothing was about to jump at him from behind. He imagined the feeling of a lion's claws sinking into his neck. The knock of the paw that would hit him over his ear. Where was he? Everything looked exactly the same. Trees heavy with snow. Fallen concrete roofs and walls on the ground, in every direction, like an immobile set of waves, waiting for a wiggle and a waggle on his part to drag him down.

He loosened the zipper of his coat, freeing his neck. He decided to find his dogs and get the hell back home. This stocktaking would have to wait. Afraid of attracting attention he tried to breathe more calmly, through the nose.

He turned around. The persistent stench of the burning carcasses and a massive pile of dung just next to him made him vomit. Through the blanket of falling snow he thought he saw a shadow, something moving. He stopped. He turned around. Nothing there. He moved a bit further and saw a slanting Perspex screen just a few metres ahead. By the screen there seemed to be some shelter from the snow. He walked over. Touching the screen he believed he saw what looked like a furry ear or a tail sticking out from a large dune-shaped heap of snow, on the other side. He scratched some ice from the Perspex to see better. The heap of snow he'd identified covered a number of animal bodies, male and female lions. Cubs. All curled tightly together. All dead. Frozen solid.

/>

<distracted

Liv sat on a hard pink puff, thinking. The Mayor, Bjørn and Kweku stood at the other end of the sparsely furnished hospital lobby, some twenty metres away, Bjørn and Kweku talking to the dayshift clerk. The snow was piling up outside the lobby's encircling floor-to-ceiling windows with a fluffy Christmassy quality. What she was thinking about was the Mayor. She wasn't sure what to think of him anymore, as in, she couldn't settle on one impression, one opinion, and therefore kept returning to him in her mind. There was something about him that made her insecure. Unsure. Along with the rest of humanity she didn't like feeling insecure, or unsure. She was impressed by him, to some extent, she reluctantly admitted, which she knew was partly the reason she felt insecure. She found his way of standing and walking absolutely assured, borderline conceited, almost to the point where she thought he might be stupid. In her experience only stupid people could carry themselves with such absolute conviction.

At the other end of the lobby Bjørn and Kweku had concluded their business with the clerk and was returning. As the Mayor followed them Liv tried to observe him more closely.

He was tall and heavy. That was a possibly distorting factor. Tallness and considerable girth, coupled with a determined disposition, had always pushed her personality assessments above the markings. It was a father thing, she knew. She couldn't see a neat Venn diagram forming around him like she wanted to. He wasn't 1/3rd innocent, 1/3rd ruthless and 1/3rd intelligent. She couldn't file him straight. That was irritating. She liked getting people into their boxes ASAP. The Mayor was more like a scatter diagram with values fired like shotgun slugs all over the place. Uncorrelatable. You couldn't draw a straight line through him and be happy it summed him up.

Though she noticed he walked without fully closing his mouth. Now that she really paid attention she also saw that his right eye wasn't all there, as in, it seemed half-dead, that the other eye seemed more alert as a consequence. With regular intervals he squinted with both eyes, as if he was deep in thought, or... just about to fall asleep? There was definitely something distant, and when she thought about it, mechanical, about the way he moved, the more she paid attention. Looking at him now she remembered how his gaze had travelled above her head the first time she spoke with him. She'd learned in interview training that this was a number one reason, a big red flag, to think multiple times about hiring someone; that someone who did that was almost certainly lying, at least being frugal with the truth. She couldn't remember if he'd ever actually met her eyes, and held them. She had a feeling he hadn't.

Coming up to her, Bjørn and Kweku sat down on the semi-circle of hard pink puffs. They put their arms on each other's backs and shook their heads solemnly. The Mayor went over to the window to check his phone's reception.

"He is here," Bjørn whispered, "Wolfgang is here. As Kweku said."

He looked at his mother, then at Kweku. Kweku was crying. His mother wasn't paying attention. She kept looking at the Mayor.

"Mamma?"

Distractedly she smiled and looked at him.

"Yes?"

"He's here, Wolfgang is *here*. They've got him. He's

in a coma. Seriously injured. He's probably not going to make it... Mamma?"

"OK," she said, having already turned towards the Mayor again.

She thought she'd seen something significant as he'd turned away, taking his phone out of his pocket, walking over to the windows and the falling snow beyond it. There'd been something in the way he'd left the group.

"Ah!"

She lifted a hand to her forehead, looking down. Finally she felt she saw what it was.

"What?" Bjørn said. "What is it?"

But she didn't answer. She just kept looking at the Mayor. She knew she really saw him now. The tall and heavy silhouette up against the uniform pattern of falling snowflakes. He was unreachable. Searching for reception. Forever would be. Pathologically distracted. Somewhere else entirely. His brain permanently wired for a 24/7 feed that had dried up. Why hadn't she noticed this before?

She felt both terrified and relieved now that she knew. A prickly heat ran up from her calves to her scalp. She started itching in unreachable places, under layers and layers of wool clothing, under her feet, down the middle of her back. A whole sequence of past events became meaningful. She felt a rush coming on and had to steady herself on the pink puff. Maybe he hadn't been lying, not directly, but she knew the promised treatment for her arms and legs would never happen. He would simply forget. The man was a goner. Out of orbit. She realised that now. He was tumbling into infinity in a state of catatonia. Probably couldn't even find his own shoes anymore. What little official backing and presence there'd been would soon be gone. She slowly turned around and looked at her son.

/>

<the_end_of_something

Bjørn was slouching by the large rickety IKEA table in the living-cum-kitchen-cum snow-removal-operations room, his ski-clothes still on, his hair sweaty and hat-shaped, feeling increasingly cold from drying his moist underwear with his own body's heat. He was repeatedly lifting an empty tumbler just above the table, then dropping it, creating a dull loud sound. The tumbler was a single promotional tumbler and therefore had a frosted silhouette of the Glenfiddich stag on its side.

Bjørn's mother and Kweku stood by the room's largest wall, sticking pins into a huge map of London, tying red string around each pin, demarcating streets already cleared of snow that week, following their schedule and Bjørn's reports.

By repetition thirty Bjørn felt he needed to exert a ridiculous amount of power lifting the tumbler. He tried to envisage the force pulling it out of his grip and back onto the table. The loud obtuse sound it made as it hit the surface felt to Bjørn, after successive repetitions, out of all proportion with what he thought of as his memory, or experience, of lifting and letting go of things similarly sized. As he held the tumbler just above the table one more time, and tried not to let go, he felt the thing slipping, being pulled out of his hand. And the more he considered the force pulling the glass down, the more awesome that power became.

He lost his grip. The tumbler smacked the table. His mother and Kweku turned around.

"Bjørn! Pleeease."

He didn't look at them, didn't look at anything in particular. His eyes lost focus. His head dropped. He folded his hands in his lap; his buttocks didn't really touch the chair, the top of his spine rested painfully against the backrest. He felt sad. The feeling spread from his chest down into his groin, then up to just above his nose. It was a feeling of not wanting to move. A vacuum-like feeling that had no clear flavour or direction. He didn't feel like he wanted anything. Didn't feel the need to do anything. He couldn't think of what he was supposed to do. Getting changed out of his wet clothes felt like work. Sitting still seemed pointless. He couldn't think of anything he wanted to eat, or drink, or watch. Of anyone he wanted to talk to. He felt he had nothing to say, at least nothing he wanted to say.

He looked at the tumbler, immobile on the table, continually pulled down onto the surface, and held still there by the same force that had pulled it out of his hand. The feeling of looking at it made him want to vomit. He closed his eyes and swallowed the spit flooding his mouth.

His mother and Kweku kept pinning pins to the enormous map of London, tying red pieces of string around them, planning tomorrow's schedule as they compared the map with driver rotas, available vehicles' current location and estimated fuel levels, though they'd both noticed that Bjørn had grown quiet and still.

Bjørn tried to force himself to think about what he'd seen that day. He needed to find something concrete, something that would push away the thought of the invisible force that exerted on the tumbler.

OK. What had he seen?

He'd seen the snow continuing to pile up. In untouched corners it already measured three metres deep. He'd seen people freezing, really freezing, shaking, being incoherent, their eyes distant and watery, almost everyone wearing way too little to stay convincingly warm. And why were they all out walking anyway? It had seemed mysterious, that so many people were out walking, freezing, with seemingly no errand, no purpose to their movements. Were they looking for phone reception? Was that it? Still? After so many months of no signal?

He'd talked to a group of young professionals, dressed in frayed pinstriped suits, over by St. Paul's station. Their feeble arms had groped for his hat and scarf. He hadn't been able to make any sense of what they'd said in-between all the teeth-clatter. Maybe they'd planned to go to the office? But no offices had been open for months.

He'd seen the sheets of ice that were clinging to most of the buildings in the City. How the snow was starting to fasten to these, turning the large vertical surfaces completely white. He'd felt like he'd been skiing through a modernist painting of abstract shapes.

Then he'd seen the smoke, black thick smoke, and groups of poorlyclads heading towards where it seemed to be coming from. It had turned out to be a fire down by London Bridge, a building he hadn't noticed before. It had crackled obliquely as it disintegrated and turned to ash. The yellow dumpers and ploughs had filed past, loudly, carrying tons of packed ice. No one was working to put the fire out. Around the burning building the snow had melted in a large radial patch, and looking at the melted darkness, in-between the whiteness all-around, had felt like looking at a large cave-entrance, a portal. And before the portal, in front of the burning fire, the men (oddly no women) had stood in a dense semi-circle, arms outstretched, warming themselves.

He'd felt he stood at the end of something then. There by London Bridge. By the burning house, looking at the semi-circle of men warming themselves. He'd felt a part of him disappear. He'd stood watching the men's shadows falling large and trembling on the white wall of the building behind them. He'd felt a sorrowful sense of saying goodbye to something he couldn't clearly name.

He'd thought very distinctly that the nervous jittery movement of the men's shadows on the wall behind them had been an image of the future. Of all the unrest waiting up ahead. All the difficulty that lay in store.

Then he'd picked up his poles and had hurried home on the frozen Thames, in long freestyle strokes.

Looking at the tumbler again, he sighed loudly. He was about to cry. He didn't want to. No. Not in front of his mother and Kweku. He could've cried in front of his mother, but not in front of them both.

He told them he had to get changed and went to his room and sat down on the bed. He left the light off, pulled the curtain aside and looked at the snow falling. This was the room his mother was now sleeping in. The double-glazed windows and the rubber insulation created a silence you could almost touch. And the muffling quality of the snow and the lack of traffic or planes or any other outside noise added to the sense Bjørn got of suddenly being in a space cut off, a space sequestered. A cell.

He lay down on the bed. He thought about how someone would portray his life in a documentary made for TV. What elements would be emphasised? Which ones played down? Which ones even neglected?

Say the director's angle would've been that he, Bjørn Olsen, had been quite naive, that he'd probably been quite selfish in may ways, making sure his needs were attended to first and foremost, his whims satisfied. Maybe not very consciously, but still, that others had found him self-centred. That angle could then form the story's narrative backbone, informing the other elements, and could perhaps creatively be dramatised as an absence. Say the director had chosen to reconstruct Bjørn's eighteenth birthday, the scene could then show his mother standing by the window looking for him, the food getting cold, the guests shaking their heads. That scene could again be chained with his sister's PhD ceremony, his mother once more looking for him in the corridor of the university, then giving up and going back in, closing the door behind her. All the while the narrator could've talked about what had made him stay away, what stupidities he'd been up to instead of showing up, and the camera could've panned across a few receipts lying on a sparsely lit table, a strip of pictures from a photo booth (him and two friends), empty beer cans, full ashtrays, to the sound of laughter and a car driving, and a song that was popular on MTV that year. Then, one could imagine an abrupt edit, a fast-forward in time, to a scene in a hotel room in Greenland, and another reconstruction. The actor chosen to represent him could be standing at the large windows, seen alternately from outside and inside the room, deep in thought, looking distractedly into the mid-distance.

The director could've told a story that way. But would it have summed him up? Been him?

He felt absolutely exhausted thinking about this. Lying on his side, curled up, his hands between his thighs, his ski-clothes still on, the duvet pulled over his shoulders, he watched the eternal snow falling outside the window. The pillow smelled of his mother's perfume.

There was a knock on the door.

"Bjørn?"

It was his mother. He took a shallow breath.

"Yes."

"Are you coming out?"

She opened the door slightly and could see his face in the narrow slit of light that came from the naked lamp in the roof behind her.

"What for?"

"We've been cooking."

"Oh."

"I thought you wanted to get changed?"

"I did."

"But you've been in here for over an hour. And you haven't changed?"

"I know."

"We wanted to cheer you up. You seemed so low earlier. We found a projector when we were out. The Bangladeshi neighbour helped us. And some DVDs."

She looked at him, smiling, raising her eyebrows.

"We found City Lights. Remember? How you loved that scene when Chaplin's a street cleaner? You remember? When the elephant comes? You loved that so much I remember. How are you? Is something the matter? Bjørn?"

She entered, closed the door behind her and disappeared in the darkness.

"No, It's nothing. I'm just tired."

"Tell me, what's the matter? You've been so quiet all evening?"

She came and sat down on the edge of the mattress and laid a hand on his shoulder.

"What is it?"

Her voice was worried and warm and kind. Bjørn felt his sadness intensify and the muscles in his throat tightening and he started crying. His mother squeezed his shoulder and moved closer and held him tight to her. She put his head in her lap and stroked his hair.

/>

<observations

The snow was falling thick over Oxford Street. It was 2.30 p.m. Probably a Thursday. The light was evenly dispersed. The snow-removal delegation was passing through town, from East to West, standing at the bridge of the Caterpillar 797F, holding their palms up to their brows to see what was going on. The Mayor was wearing his wool-insulated wellingtons. His red hunting cap was pulled hard down over his ears. His globular head looked over-ripe, infected. His dark-green Barbour jacket hung stiff and heavy on his shoulders, creaking when he lifted an arm. He was silent, looked sad, checking his phone for signal.

There was havoc. There was manic movement all around them. There wafted thick desperation through the air, along with the black rancid smoke from multiple cars on fire. Liv held her scarf in front of her nose. Bjørn snapped pictures of a hooded teenage girl entering an Agent Provocateur through one of its broken windows. As the girl disappeared into the shop, five older women came out into the snow, carrying what they could of lace stockings, thongs, briefs and bras, stuffed tightly into plastic bags. Further down the street another five hooded figures kicked at the window of a parked Mercedes. The glass bent like crystallised layers of honeycomb, but it didn't give, not completely. Then they ran off. Snowballs flew in every conceivable direction. There was loud shouting, even through the muffling snow and the roar of the dumper's engine. Barrel and crate-sized objects were lifted and thrown into the few shop-windows still intact. Liv pointed ahead of them to the Top Shop on Oxford Circus. It was on fire – mad synthetic fire. Its flames were spreading towards Nike. The H&M across the junction was no longer an H&M in any conventional sense. It was an empty burnt-out shell. For no apparent reason people were scaling its façade. People on the ground were pummelling the people climbing with snowballs. One of the climbers fell down from the fourth floor, hitting the pavement, and didn't get up again. Nobody seemed to care. It was snowing so thickly you wondered if you would be able to breathe for much longer. Unbelievably, seagulls were circling in the air above, quietly through the snow.

It felt like they were keeping score, tracing and recording the randomness with their persistent movements. Maybe they were writing something on the fabric of time?

The monumental dumper moved slowly forward, turned through the scurrying masses into Regent Street, past the skeletal remains of what were once the shops Monsoon, COS, Jaeger and Hamley's. At Hamley's one of the army officers started crying as he saw a lone scruffy Paddington Bear hanging from a charred flagpole. He imagined the bear trying to save itself, climbing. He thought he actually saw it move, stretching for safety on a nearby ledge. But then it fell into the crowd, was torn to pieces, and the officer gasped as the crowd jeered.

From there the dumper took a turn down Maddox Street, and driving loudly down towards Bond Street it shook loose an avalanche that came off the roof of the building that once, many years ago, was a branch of the Northern Rock bank. Luckily the five tons of snow only hit the hind-parts of the enormous vehicle, shaking it hard, but not tipping it over.

Brushing the dust of snow from her hair, Liv asked the driver to take them back to the Russell Hotel again. She thought it had been more than enough for one day already. In any case, she had a speech to write for the evening.

/>

<talking_to_the_void

"OK everyone… here, welcome, also if you can see it on your computer, wherever you are, listen, sorry if my English is a bit so so, but you will know what I mean."

Liv stood wide and heavy on the small podium in the Russell Hotel's breakfast room, just in front of the kitchen entrance. She was wearing a black Chanel suit, some simple jewellery around her arms and neck. Between her words and under the humming feedback from the speakers the crowd of delegation officials could hear the occasional sound of dishes being stacked and water being turned on and off. It was late evening. The light was dim, except for where Liv stood. At the front Bjørn and Kirsty looked up, expectantly. The Mayor was checking his mobile for signal. The Norwegian Ambassador whispered something to his secretary, smiling dully. Everyone else was quiet.

"Ladies and Gentlemen, this is a crisis, I am sure you know. Today on our tour through London, yes we, you and I, saw the effect for real. I am not one for the sentimental pausing, normally, but we have to recognise the human suffering element. So far we have focused too much on the snow, I feel."

Her eyes scanned the row of heads with intensity, demanding affirmation, attention. Kweku was filming her from the back of the room, the single red light glowing in the dark, streaming the performance live through the University of London's historical Ethernet, and from there hopefully further, with the help of student ingenuity.

"I stood there by the Thames today, next to you, and it struck me, it struck me that we do not know anything about this, and we have to be OK with that, I mean, we have to accept that we are in a weak position with this snow, to do the best we can with what we have, to plan day-by-day, perhaps week-by-week, if we are lucky. "

She cleared her throat, crossed her arms and squeezed her shoulders in pain. Then she clutched her hands in front of her chest, holding her upper abdomen, the jewellery making a small metallic noise over the PA system.

"As I said, I am here to help remove the snow, that

is my expertise. But today I saw something else that made me think, once more. There is so much of it. I felt so hopeless today. And helpless, to be honest. I am not afraid to say it. I did. We have to be able to say how we feel. I am a believer from our feelings we can know a lot. Right Mr Mayor?"

She looked down at the Mayor and the Norwegian Ambassador. They felt her gaze and both looked up, sheepishly. Then the Mayor nodded and turned to his phone again.

"It made me sad today and I think we need to remember that many people will be very sad right now. Tonight. Lonely. What is tomorrow like? Next week? We don't know. For many years we have lived so well, most of us. Now is a different situation, it seems. I felt this for the first time today. It made me very sad, that we should live through this, in our lifetime."

A big crash of plates was heard from the kitchen.

"But we are. As other nations and other times have seen worse, for sure. But this is us now. Now we are here. Facing this. You and I. This is our brief time given a new perspective, a new light, or less of it. And a lot more snow than we expected. I am not religious. If you are I am happy for you. It is not my business. If it helps you find strength, then good. But do not preach, please."

She scanned the rows of heads and smiled at them all, melancholy, wisely. She paused for a while, looked into the middle-distance, into the dimness.

"Today I saw many homeless people frozen to death over by Tate Modern, I saw families with children chopping up their furniture to burn in barrels. I saw five men fighting over a frozen banana. I saw buildings burning everywhere. I heard people screaming at each other, non-stop. So many were drunk, so many, so many. Also, so many were high, too many. I saw someone in their home, through the window, tearing up books to burn. I saw all this today. We saw it together. And I saw all the empty streets, all the abandoned cars, and I thought I must not despair. I must not. We must find a way to deal with this."

The Norwegian Ambassador checked his mobile, turned to whisper to his secretary, looked at the decorations around the base of the column next to him, then smiled his vacant smile again, scratching his nose, looking at nothing in particular. Bjørn saw him in the corner of his eye and felt a cold draft passing his legs, like a door just swung open to a dungeon, wet and slimy. The Mayor yawned, then checked his phone.

"What brought us here I will not speculate. Too many theories, too many factors. Now is time for action, not blaming. In our time of most worry we must be clear and active. Maybe some day we will know, or if someone comes after us, they will. As I believe they will, someone must come after us. I want that. I want someone to come after us and say we did something right. As I believe there is something to fight for, in life. I have always believed so. Something to keep about us humans. Something we share, something good about us. Something worth preserving. Even if I am very sad today. It is a feeling I have. I hope you can see and feel it too. I hold fast to this feeling. This idea. Don't let despair crawl all over you, as we say where I come from. I find comfort in sharing the same destiny with you. We will all go the same way, some day, but I want us to pass that opportunity on. I urge you to help me give the children a chance, at living a life. It is bigger than us. Excuse my sentiment, but, I find life so very sweet, too sweet often, that I want to share it. It is too much for me. Alone. Too big. I don't want to be one person in the last generation who tasted it this way."

A trolley full of biscuits and tinned fruits appeared in the door behind her, the Bangladeshi waiter pushing it concentrating hard, then another trolley with more of the same, its Bangladeshi waiter behind. Realising they were both in full view of the crowd they stopped for a moment and smiled, confused, then walked hurriedly back into the kitchen. A loud bang and rattle was heard as the door swung through the frame and hit the last trolley.

"Please Ladies and Gentlemen, here in this hotel tonight, and at home, or wherever you are, if you can see this, we saw so much unhappiness today, so much sorrow and despair, but please let us not forget that we must work to do our best now, to clear the snow, and we must find some of our self-respect again. We must."

A short burst of clapping peaked, then died.

"Thank you for that, but remember, now is when the work starts. Now is when we will find out what we are made of. I hope it is good stuff. I hope it is what I believe in. Goodnight."

Liv closed her eyes and held them shut for a long while, listening to the crowd clapping, then dispersing, the Mayor and the Norwegian Ambassador starting a conversation. Bjørn turned around to the back and made a movement with his right hand across his neck, as if to cut it. Kweku switched the camera off.

/>

/alone

Started at Tue Sep 19 02:58:26 27020

Command line was: ./henkick_1265 --out-dir=store/
final_rebuild --out-postfix=arx_run_0_no_clean
--creat-sigma=10 --no-plot --save-plot --kwg-
base=hk_kwg_9.db --drives-list=drives.txt --drive-
idx=104

Version tag 3.12.1.1265, built Sat Tue 19 02:58:23
27020

Job ID is: 152838, 1502 instances allocated

VC hash: d536dfa944fb

parsing recovered files at /store/recovery/drvA7S

<from_space

Peering at it from the outer depths of the universe, the Earth looked like it did billions of years ago, if one had been able to spot its microscopic presence among the brightness of all the billion trillions of stars. The light it reflected back then, in its infancy, was only now reaching out there, so infinitely far away. It looked different then, very different. Not yet fully formed. Darker, yellow and red in patches, blue stormy oceans, and no green. But moving closer in, through the billions of galaxies, observing it nearer and nearer, it grew older. Stopping at 1 billion light years away its neighbouring superclusters of stars became visible, like fatty smudges on a dark window: Virgo, Hydra, Leo, Centaurus, Pisces. Still invisible, in any meaningful sense of the word, the Earth, in there, among the bright lights, looked like it did 1 billion years ago, the supercontinent Rodinia forming. And moving closer towards it at the speed of light, it progressively appeared as it did as it got older, year by year, month by month, day by day, for 1 billion years; mountain-chains rising and eroding, rising and eroding, other supercontinents forming, breaking apart and reforming, breaking apart and reforming again. The oceans changing their shapes across the globe, over and over, for millions and millions of years, by the speed of a fingernail growing. This movement through the universe towards the Earth was a movement past innumerable galaxies, themselves hundreds of thousands of light-years apart, and within each galaxy unfathomable distances between individual stars, a movement which, if it was animated and sped up, looked like moving inside a snowstorm, the spiral galaxies like individual snowflakes. A storm of falling stars in space. At a hundred million light years away, moving towards the Earth, the Milky Way was not even a pinprick on the firmament. Still moving for another 95 million years, forever really, through the emptiness of space, forever and ever, past the age of dinosaurs, and coming to a halt, observing the Earth from 5 million light-years away, its home galaxy finally appeared as a tiny disk, far to the left of Andromeda. There, there was the Milky Way! And travelling on, for millions of years, still observing the Earth, it grew older and older, species of animals and plants appeared and became extinct, again and again, over and over. Then the first modern humans appeared at a distance of 200 hundred thousand light years away. Flying past the Magellanic clouds and its Tarantula nebula, the earth appeared as it was 170 thousand years ago. And from 50 thousand light years away the Milky Way lay there ahead, a vortex of light and gas, the sun a speck somewhere in the brightness. Then ice ages came and went. By the time of the Egyptian civilisation, the sun became faintly visible, just to the right of Betelgeuse, in there amongst Polaris, Rigel and the Orion nebula. By the time of the French revolution, Vega appeared, Aldebaran, the stars of Ursa Major. By World War two the solar system took shape ahead. And still moving on, closer and closer to Earth, at the time of the last American presidential election, four years ago, Proxima Centauri twinkled past, the closest star apart from the Sun. And there it was, faintly visible, blue and white, the Earth. Moving towards it past the other planets it appeared almost as old as it had ever been, a few years ago only, and moving closer, as close to it as the sun, eight minutes away, it appeared to have lost its blue colour. It appeared white, white all over. Past the moon it was obvious that the cover of clouds was thick. And moving through the white, to the underside of the clouds, it was snowing, heavy, continuously. And down through the air, over London, coming down to the ground, it became clear that it had been snowing for a while. The layer on the ground had grown at least a couple of metres thick. And there was St. Thomas' hospital below. And in a room on the third floor, was Wolfgang, lying in bed, unconscious. And finally it was the present.

/>

<the_happiest_moment

He'd felt a sense of relief as the ferry had pulled out of Calais harbour. Fredrik, his old friend, who'd helped him move to Berlin the last time, had gone into the tax-free shop and Wolfgang was sitting alone at one of the bolted-down tables with a view to the side of the ship. The heavy rain that had followed them from Antwerp had stopped and although the sea was going quite high, the sky looked like the sun would peek through very soon. He sighed heavily from a great swirling anticipation in his stomach. A stupid kind of smile settled on his round face.

Moving to London. What lay ahead now?

A big wave rolled under the ship and a group of pension-ers, weekday daytime shoppers he assumed, moved in unison across the ship's floor like prawns tossed in a frying pan. It seemed choreographed somehow, and funny, and made Wolfgang think that maybe all movement was like this, like some great wave of sorts was always tossing people about in groups.

What kind of wave was he being moved by then? And who were being moved in unison with him? He couldn't think of anything more specific than maybe a thirst-for-knowledge wave, or a general-opportunity wave. Or maybe there was such a thing as a more specific technology wave? He felt his body tugged backwards by the undulating sea. Perhaps there was a wave particular to those who studied the physics of weather? That thought made him laugh. But then he stopped laughing. His face grew serious and thoughtful.

Wouldn't they all be moved by the same larger wave although they personally might belong to other smaller waves? And how could that be possible? How could all these different waves not start cancelling each other?

He felt confused and all of a sudden irritated by his efforts to apply physical theory to other things than particles in vacuum.

But then what was the point of studying physics?

Well. Nearly everything around him was a result of some kind of scientific theory put into practice, the boat for one, the hardened glass windows, the cushioned seat he was sitting on. Studying physics had changed the world and was changing it faster now than at any other time in human history. It worked. It was a successful enterprise.

The problem was the alluring possibility that the laws of physics should also be able to explain human behaviour and motivation. But beyond the simplest analogy of the wave, the experiment collapsed. Human thoughts and actions were almost impossible to classify beyond very basic motivations. He knew that psychiatry and psychology had tried, but still basically failed.

His mother had always talked about a wave of love extending from the heart. A wave of love emitting from all humans, even in the bleakest of times. That love was the true essence of who we were, the real life-force. He'd always found that corny.

But what if she'd been right? Where did love come from then? Who started love? Was love a wave? Or particles? Or both? Did it have a prime mover?

In his experience when two people got together their misunderstandings magnified each conflict, as had happened with Jana.

There was a good use of the wave-analogy. Two people doubling their grief when they were put together in the same room, if they kept on misunderstanding each other. And then cancelling each other if they were too similar? Too good to each other? No. That didn't compute.

He caught a glimpse of another boat in the distance and figured it was a container-carrier. His thoughts came out from the backrooms of his mind. He remembered where he was. Where he was going. The sun came through in a solid yellow beam onto the surface of the water. The ocean was green and grey and foamy in the bright light. His guts did a kneading movement. Did he need the toilet?

He drew a long breath of air through his nose and blew it out again through his mouth.

What was the happiest moment of his life?

He thought back on the last years in Berlin, most of them spent with Jana. Were they the happiest? Some of them? A few days? Maybe. But he couldn't commit to the thought and felt that either he knew without hesitation or else he didn't. But that meant he possibly didn't know when he'd been the happiest?

He knew when he'd been the saddest. That was easy. The last months with Jana. The weeks after his grandfather had died. His first year in Berlin.

He felt like the fleeting happy moments he'd experienced had all bled into one shiny spot on the retina, no longer distinguishable from each other, too bright, as when you massaged your eyeballs through the lids and let go.

But the sad periods stayed. He went back to them and relived them, they came into his dreams, gave his nightmares colour and shape. He tried to figure out what had gone wrong, over and over, he regretted something he'd said, wished he'd done something differently.

What was the physiological reason that pain was remembered better than bliss? If he took his experience at face value the implication seemed to be that there was nothing to learn from happiness. To be happy seemed to be the neutral state of the organism, when the flight-recorder was turned off, when the body could afford to bask effortlessly at sea level. The state of happiness was not made to be remembered; it was made to give a respite from the other stuff, the coping, the hassle, the organising, the worrying.

But being sad was hard work. Experiences that remained unexplained demanded re-examination. He tried to learn from them but the lessons always eluded him, at least it felt that way.

From his recent studies the most exhilarating experiences had all come to him when he'd been in deep concentration, when he'd had a sense of glimpsing larger connections (several books open on his desk), a structure beyond what was immediately apparent. In those moments he'd felt peaceful, intensely focused. It hadn't felt like work. It had been fun to learn. He'd felt completely switched on, humming along. Hours had disappeared.

He'd read about these moments described as flow. The word somewhat covered his experience, he could see what it was getting at, but it had felt more like climbing up from a gully of flow and into a space where things were stationary, still, everywhere present all at once, extending and coming back at the same time.

So maybe these few experiences while studying had been the happiest of his life? At least he remembered them. He hadn't felt torn then, not distracted and unproductive. At the mercy of his wants. Though he knew he'd become the same miserable unsatisfied self again as soon as he'd shut the books.

Happiness seemed linked both to total mindlessness and complete mindfulness, where the first was a holiday from negative experience, from the school of life, and the other the most pleasurable form of learning. One could hardly be recalled – the moments blending into a nothingness, the other could be intensely remembered – but then in sharp contrast to the dull existence either side of it.

A few pensioners stumbled past, their steps short and tentative. Their heads looked much lighter than younger people's. A tremble in their hands was quite visible. Their arms hung sort of drugged and immobile by their sides. Their whitewashed hair, clean like moss, or ash.

Was happiness the wrong measure of happiness? Was contentedness better? A prolonged sense of feeling more than usually at ease and confident? On the right path? As opposed to periods in his life when he'd felt he was going nowhere, stagnating, angry, out of character, depressed almost?

It seemed like contentedness was connected to being on track, to seeing progression, to forward motion, whereas depression was almost always in his experience linked to stopping up, to going nowhere, to going down a dead end.

In that case, feeling content was defined by his understanding of what the right path was. It was linked to an idea of himself as a future someone, a future someone who'd arrived somewhere specific, who'd done something of specific value on his way there.

His sense of self, his sense of being happy with what he currently was, in the most basic definition, was measured against this blueprint of a journey through life. Where had the blueprint come from? Who had hung it in his head? What were the options available? The neighbouring connecting versions of the map? Or could he only see this one? Was that what people referred to as fate?

Another thick sunbeam appeared in the distance, like a funnel, from cloud to ocean. A group of gulls became illuminated as they flew through it. It looked tactile and powerful. The water where the beam met the surface glowed a coppery kind of green, the whitecaps a light yellow. Wolfgang felt his mind pause somehow, looking at this, as if he'd stopped thinking. Then the beam disappeared.

Jana had become a Buddhist before they'd split up and he had for a few months toyed with the option himself. It seemed such a simple yet hard and therefore powerful strategy. It consisted of subjugating one's thoughts, was his take on it, of conditioning body and mind to function as much as possible outside the context and motion of random daily life and thereby freeing oneself from feeling worried and anxious. As he thought of it now it reminded him of the first form of happiness, the blissful yet ignorant one. And perhaps that was what he'd instinctively felt when he chose not to follow Jana into Buddhism? That he wanted a conscious, but still troubled state? That he needed his neurosis? That he somehow wanted to feel connected to his time? No matter how shitty it was?

He couldn't cut the ties to his blueprint. And his was a German one, drawn under specific conditions, by growing up in a family dominated by a deeply religious mother, and so on. He felt allegiances he didn't see Jana having. His feeling was very distinctly that she was not being true to her place, in the grander scheme of things. Her Buddhism had felt inauthentic. He knew this could be perceived as arrogant, by someone reading his thoughts (for instance), for why was she inauthentic and he authentic?

He couldn't say why he felt that way. He just did. He could be wrong, he was aware of that. He was aware that Jana could be the one acting authentically, in accordance with a better blueprint, a more harmonic one, less obsessed with improving herself in her own image, but more concerned with helping life all 'round. Less selfish. But to Wolfgang her Buddhism was just as selfish as his decision to pursue a PhD in economics, on top of his degree in physics.

He felt good looking out at the green, foamy ocean. He felt easy, sitting there waiting for Fredrik to return from the tax-free shop. He'd broken out from Berlin, from Germany. He'd cut the ropes. Followed what he thought he wanted. He did feel present there in that seat, looking out at the white-capped ocean, the upturned Ws of seagulls in the distance. The feeling was connected to the kneading anticipation working in his stomach. It was hopeful. In an hour they would dock at the port of Dover, headed for London.

/>

<voracious

[syntax error: possible scrambled file]
Did Jana also remember how the spider was catching more insects than it could ever eat, how it moved so frantically about the light-bulb, how its legs were shining in the light from that bulb behind it when it curled them around the edge of the box that held the light and how the insects kept flying into that box and how they'd bent down to look at it and how no one else cared about what they were looking at, but that they cared deeply and were both fascinated and a little horrified by the manic activity around that single light bulb, there in the heart of the summer-night, out there in the fields north of Berlin, how they'd wondered if the spider would eat all the insects that night or save some for later, or if other animals or insects would come

and take away some of those moths wrapped in spider-silk, and did she sometimes remember the chirruping of the frogs and how Wolfgang's heart had raced when his foot got entangled in a water-lily when they went swimming, how she felt his neck and laughed when she could feel the quick pumping of blood around his body, how that also made her feel more in love with him, she'd said, that she'd called him her Prince then, how Wolfgang was trying to see if he could dry in the middle of the night by simply lying on one of the bathing-chairs, but became too cold and started shivering and talked incoherently, and how he at the same time kept both eyes on the night-sky, the black glove speckled with rhinestone pulled onto the hand and arm of the heaven, and how he'd pointed it out to her and how she'd said she thought the sky at night looked like the moment just after a single firework element had exploded, the embers of the firework blowing away for a short short moment, and then going black, but how the stars were just the same embers from that initial firework she'd just learned about at university, the class Wolfgang had encouraged her to take, in fact he was the one who'd made her go back to school again, did she remember – that without Wolfgang she would perhaps just be working at Lidl still, drinking coffee with her roommates and discussing the way the world worked without really having any idea what she was talking about, and how on that night Jana had somehow thanked Wolfgang for encouraging her to go back to school, and then to university, just by the way she'd shared his enthusiasm for the things around them, for all the things around them, for the radical mystery of the things that surrounded them and how much pleasure they gave them when they really looked at them, how she thanked him he felt, just by saying what she'd said, how the stars were embers from the initial burst, although not strictly right somehow more right than all the other theories about stars Wolfgang had ever read, how he was lying there naked next to her on the wooden deck-chair beside the muggy-smelling lake they'd just taken a swim in, and did she remember how Wolfgang had stretched his arm out to take hers in his then, how happy he was that she was there with him, how he hoped he really really hoped she knew and sometimes thought about and remembered that moment in the almost total darkness, that night they studied the voracious spider and listened to the call of those frogs they couldn't see.

/>

Wolfgang Ender <wolfgang.ender@gmail.com>Sun, Jul 25, 2010 at 2:07 PM
Subject: Long time

Dear Jana,

I just wanted to tell you that both my parents passed away this spring and early summer. Since you met them a few times I thought you would like to know.
I am in Altensteig now in the house you visited. I am fine. Dealing with the things you have to deal with I suppose, practical things mostly, about the house and so on. You can't imagine all the toilet prototypes my father kept in the cellar, after my grandfather (If you remember?).

I hope you are well. Would be nice to know what you are
up to these days. I still live in London. Going back the
day after tomorrow.

W.

/>

<stansted_airport

"Fredrik, is that you?"

Wolfgang held the mobile phone hard against his right ear while covering his left. The coffee-shop chatter was too loud for him to hear what the person was saying. Most of the immediate noise came from a family of three next to him, mother and father entertaining their young son by constantly hiding and revealing their faces. This had been going on since Wolfgang had sat down, about ten minutes ago. The kid actually looked tired by now, about to cry.

"Fredrik? Hello?"

"Hello?"

"Hello, can you hear me?"

"Who is this?"

The voice in Wolfgang's ear sounded like it turned away from the phone and spoke to someone else in the room.

"It's Wolfgang... Is that you Fredrik?"

The voice in the other end was still talking to someone else. Then it went silent and returned to the phone.

"Wolfgang Ender?"

The child next to Wolfgang started crying and both parents were waving their hands, laughing and making silly noises. For a second the child looked surprised, then amused, then terrified. Its face went red. Then it started crying louder than before.

"Yes, Wolfgang Ender... Fredrik?"

"No."

"Oh, I'm sorry. Is Fredrik there?"

The voice turned away from the phone again and spoke to someone else. Wolfgang got up. He left his table with a half-drunk cup of coffee on it. Holding his bag in place with his left elbow he managed to still cover his ear and hold the phone tight with the other hand. He walked fast towards what looked like a quieter corner of the waiting lounge, behind some pillars.

"Wolfgang...?"

"Yes... Wolfgang, Wolfgang from school."

Wolfgang recognised Fredrik's father's voice now, though it was much feebler than he remembered it, more cracked, like old porcelain. A beeping vehicle carrying an old lady passed by. He went around the pillar while he tried with all his power to hear if the other person on the line was saying something.

"Is Fredrik there?"

He almost shouted.

"Your parents, we are sorry."

"Thank you, that's kind."

"Fredrik would have come to the funeral we are sure, but we were too old by now."

He was standing by the entrance to the toilets. The loud sound of hand-driers kept reaching him and dying away.

"So Fredrik isn't there?"

"We are sure he would have come."

Wolfgang felt the effects of adrenalin flowing into his bloodstream. Had something happened to his old friend?

"Mr. Jankowitz, please..."

"We talked about you Wolfgang."

At least five hand-driers started at the same time, forcing Wolfgang around the pillar again.

"Mr. Jankowitz... Where is Fredrik?"

"Hello?"

"Yes, hello, Mr. Jankowitz. Is Fredrik there? Is he at home?"

Wolfgang felt as if something was sharpening in him.

"Fredrik is not here."

The voice turned aside again, Wolfgang guessed to Fredrik's mother, to confer. His heartbeat was making him feel like his hands had a life of their own.

"Mr. Jankowitz, is Fredrik... Where is he?"

The voice of Fredrik's father stopped conferring with the other person in the room. Wolfgang thought he heard the sound of a wall-mounted clock striking the half-hour.

"Wolfgang, we thought you knew. Fredrik lives in Thailand."

The rush of relief was immediate, followed by a feeling of being both angry and hurt. He wanted to shout something obscene. Why had he thought he'd be in his childhood home anyway? He knew he probably hadn't lived there for years. When was the last time they'd spoken? He couldn't remember. They'd lost touch shortly after Wolfgang had moved to London. It was absurd. How could he have called, and then kept pestering Fredrik's parents for so long, without realising? Was his mind slipping? It seemed perhaps he'd needed Fredrik to still be there, living in his parent's home, the way it had been when they were boys, now that he had no connection back there anymore. And Fredrik was living in Thailand? And why had it taken the old parents so long to spit it out? Was there something unusual about the situation? From a German middle-class perspective? Was he living with a man? A she-male? Not that he cared, in any case. It was the same to him. He would be happy for him, as long as he was happy. But if true, if his old friend was living a life his parents were trying their best to hide from the world, it only went to show how little Wolfgang had paid attention. How little he'd been aware of people around him. Focusing so intensely on his own path.

He looked at the people in front of him, moving languidly between the shops of the waiting lounge, dressed in shorts and flip-flops, some even wearing straw-hats. The hall was almost full to capacity. It felt like it couldn't handle more people before something he couldn't imagine would happen, some kind of break-down, some kind of violence. Where could he go where he would feel OK?

"I am sorry to have disturbed you Mr. Jankowitz."

"We are sorry about your parents Wolfgang."

"Thank you. Goodbye Mr. Jankowitz. Give my best to your wife."

The line went silent. He imagined the old Jankowitz couple in their living room, turning to each other, Fredrik's mother asking about the call, what Wolfgang had wanted. He saw them standing in the doorframe waving to Fredrik and Wolfgang as they backed out the drive-way in the VW going to Berlin. How long ago was that now? Fifteen? Twenty years? When was the last time he had seen them?

The anger left him. In its place he felt deeply empty. Vacuumed. He felt heavy too, despite the feeling of emptiness. He thought about Jana. How could an empty shell be so heavy? He wanted to cry. But then what good would crying do? And here? And who was there now? Who could he call? He looked at his phone. He knew he had no numbers to anyone he could call and talk to – to anyone that would make him feel better. No one in his current life had known him or seen him with his parents, except for Jana, but she was no longer in his life. She hadn't been in his life for over eight years. He kept thinking about her every day these days. He imagined her breasts. He imagined her hair as she whisked it away from her forehead. Since his parents died he imagined having sex with her almost every hour of the day. It made him feel so sad, but still he thought about her. He lifted his bag from between his feet and walked into the men's. The cubicle at the very end of the narrow and long room was free. The driers kept going on and off. He closed the door, put his bag down. He took off his jacket and hung it on the hook on the door. Doors to other cubicles were shutting and opening. Toilets were flushing. He undid his belt and the fly of his trousers and dropped them to the floor and sat down. He started crying. He imagined Jana's breasts. With his hand under his shirt, between his legs, forcing his penis down into the bowl, so as not to cast suspicious shadows, he started masturbating.

/>

<Berlin_zoo

Why was he back at the zoo? He wasn't sure. He'd been in the neighbourhood for a climate conference. He'd more or less just responded to a vague emotion, an impulse, though he knew it had to do with his last visit with Jana. How much time had passed since then? He couldn't really tell, but it was years. Almost ten years? Yes, maybe as many as ten years.

He started walking the route he thought he remembered they'd walked last time – but it was summer and the animals were outside and he couldn't really remember, so he just walked aimlessly about.

The lions were asleep under a tree. The tigers were sleeping too, under cover of a wooden barrel that had been hung up for their entertainment. The chimpanzees were dosing, lying on their backs and scratching themselves in an absentminded way. The long-haired Orang-utan held its head in its hand, its arm resting on its knee. Small birds from surrounding Berlin flew in and out of the great ape's cage, using its drinking water as their pool. They seemed to be having a great time.

Whereas, wherever Wolfgang went, the locked-up animals seemed almost depressed, or at least he felt they were.

Maybe he was just anthropomorphising? He knew he had a tendency to do it, like most people. But nonetheless, he couldn't shake the feeling. The animals seemed utterly bored. And rightly so, he thought. Their cages were being cleaned for them. Their food was being brought every day at the same time. And in between? What was there to do?

One of the chimpanzees had looked at him with such melancholy that he couldn't stand it; he'd had to walk on, shaking his head. One of two brown bears had stood on the same spot for minutes, looking like someone had hit it with a bouncy ball. It had probably slept too much. But this was summer. It shouldn't be sleeping now.

The giant rhinoceros trotted around in a large figure of eight. The pelicans, which seemed free to fly away at any time (he couldn't see any shackles or net), just sat on the rocks and looked ruffled, unclean. Bored. The elephants stood still, their giant eyelids closing and opening now and then. The emu looked like it couldn't even be bothered to look bored. The sea-lions were inactive, dosing in a corner.

As Wolfgang walked around, and as the park filled up with more and more people, he found himself looking at them instead, more and more intently, and becoming increasingly intrigued by what he was seeing. Here too was an animal, of course, and a mammal at that, and what a banal realisation. But how difficult it was to remember and hold that thought, once it occurred.

He saw families eating ice cream, large organised groups following an umbrella held high. Some were crying, some smiling, others talking, pointing, joking. Wolfgang felt as though he had never looked at people before. He broke into an instant sweat. NO, he thought. I'm not an animal. And then: of course, I am! And these people – when they looked at him, they saw the same thing he saw looking at them: just another person, among so many. Undistinguishable really. No, not even really, but absolutely. It was a banal line of realisation, he knew, but it had never hit him as hard.

He found a bench and sat down. Maybe it was a conse-quence of missing Jana? It had been a mistake coming here, looking for what he didn't know, following an impulse, happening to be in the neighbourhood for the conference. Time had passed and instead of seeing a glimpse of before he saw the relentless quality of change. Zoos should be banned. What good were they? What purpose did they serve? And what if they were banned? How would we relate to animals then? Did we actually need zoos? In order to imagine a wilderness? Did these animals do a great job of reminding him he was just like them? Was that their purpose? Or, were they simply entertainment? Ice-cream and two play-fighting polar bears at three in the afternoon?

He knew there were scientific arguments for observing animals. But was there a moral one too? For keeping them in here? Bored out of their skins?

Jana – where was she now? He missed her. It had been a mistake coming back here.

The sun broke through the clouds and he felt warm sitting on that bench in his only suit, a winter-suit made of wool. Why had he left her? He knew he was just a regular guy. OK, he had a good head, for abstract reasoning and so on, but other than that he was as square as a box. And despite this, or perhaps precisely because of this mix, he had taken off in search of something else, something more. To realise his potential. But what was his real potential? What was his real quality? Other than just being a mammal? He felt like a self. He was a self. He tought in terms of it. But he had definitely overvalued the importance of this self, to the extent that he'd left the only other person he'd ever loved, the only other mammal, apart from his mother and grandfather.

But maybe if they'd remained together he would've hated it? There was definitely that possibility. And then what? A divorce? Wasn't a break-up after several years of living together much worse? He'd never tried, so he didn't know. He had no way of knowing. He'd sought to realise his potential, sought immortality through a process that would make him distinguishable from the rest. To stand apart. To be seen by everyone else and therefore transcend mortality, or at least the feeling of having lived for nothing, without ever having reached that goal of one's own potential. People despised each other. Couldn't stand the sight of each other. Were envious. Wanted what others had and felt inadequate, nervous, restless.

But people also sometimes felt happy. There was an energy there, in him, in everyone, he supposed, that was stronger than almost everything else. A real capacity for joy.

He was deep in thought sitting on that bench. A child came up to him and put a hand, sticky with ice cream, on his knee. He looked into the child's eyes and was somehow sucked back out again, from inside the doldrums of his mind – into the soft light of the late morning.

He smiled.

The child lost its balance and fell onto its cushioned bum. It didn't cry. He bent forward to lift it up but the mother was there first. He sat back again on the bench and felt awkward. He smiled at the mother who didn't smile back but quickly walked away with the child.

Did she think he was a pervert? Was that what everyone thought of single men smiling at children?

He should really stop trying to find scraps of his old self in places he'd visited with Jana. He was tired of feeling melancholy. Maybe the animals weren't bored at all? Maybe it was just him?

</>

<round_table

"Excuse me Mr. Prime Minister..."

"Yes...?"

"Wolfgang Ender, Chair in Socio-Climatic-Impact Studies at Center for Climate Studies, London School of Economics."

"Go ahead Mr. Ender."

The fifteen members of the round-table forum looked intensely down at their personal notepads, placed on the oblong table, including the Chancellor of the Exchequer and Lord Strict, the forum's leader or head or chair. Wolfgang had interrupted the Prime Minister's keynote speech after just five minutes.

"Sorry for interrupting Sir..."

"Not a problem Mr. Ender. After all you are supposed to be the experts here, right?"

The Prime Minister smiled a wide smile without showing any teeth.

"Yes, sir, I find your introduction is very entertaining, peoples will emigrate and so on, lose electricity for weeks, maybe months, all that is very stimulating to think about, but for one moment let me..."

There was some heavy rustling of papers from over by Lord Strict. Coffee cups were being compulsively emptied all around and for many the pattern of the room's curtains had become captivatingly fascinating.

"Mr. Ender..."

Lord Strict was giving Wolfgang a very stern look.

"No please Mr. Ender... please continue," the Prime Minister insisted.

"Lord Strict, thank you Mr. Prime Minister, Changer of the Exchanger Mr. Maroon."

Forum member's faces were increasingly warm and showing it. Incomprehensible scribbling was going on. Lower leg muscles were tightened almost to the point of tearing.

"Let's say this is a perspective from a longer view. Let's say this is a view from let's say twenty thousand years ago. From the last ice age."

"OK, yes...?"

The Prime Minister was still wearing the wide smile

from a few moments ago. His assistant was indicating time running with a pointed index at his watch.

"OK, so, just this one thought, from twenty thousand years ago and let's say until the year 27000, twenty-five thousands years from now. And four words: sun storms, and the earth's core. What is the frame-works we are to see this change within, this climate changing? What time spans?"

"Mr. Ender, thank you, we will have to…"

"Sorry, just one last thing…"

The room was positively buzzing with uncomfortableness.

"You say we must preserve something for future generations. My questions is what? How we chose? And do you think it is possible to preserve anything, in the light of ice-ages and sun storms? Most seriously educated guesses say…"

"Mr. Prime Minister. We are sorry for the interruption, but Mr. Ender is a very passionate…"

"Not at all. I find the perspective refreshing. Thank you Mr. Ender. If I can, though, pick up where I?"

"Excuse me Mr. Prime Minister, just the one more thing…"

"Mr. Ender, I have to ask you to…"

Lord Strict had put on his glasses and was looking straight at Wolfgang.

"Our best educated guesses are as good or bad as hot air, sir, excuse the puns. What is your story for the masses of people? That they can makes a difference?"

The Prime Minister had switched to his next slide and was looking at it, still smiling.

"As I was saying…"

Lord Strict was whispering into the ear of a large black man squatting by his side. They both looked at Wolfgang, who took a sip of water and smiled as he looked at the colourful slide somehow pulsating on the wall ahead of them.

/>

<mother

[memetic error: possible scrambled file]
Was Wolfgang dreaming? Was that snow outside the window? What was this thing ahead of him? Why was he following it? Who were these men? Why did they sit next to his bed? Why was he in bed? Where was this bed? What was that around his arm? Why couldn't he move his legs? Were his eyes open? Was this one of those lucid dreams? Where he tried to wake up? But couldn't? Really, what was this big dark thing in the corner of the room? It seemed sad. Could big dark objects be sad? It looked like it had run out of steam. It looked tired. But how could a large dark sort of round object be tired? And what was it doing there? What was he doing there? Who were these men leaning over his bed? Why was one of them touching

his eyelid? Was he squeezing his hand? Was that his helmet over there, next to the big black sad round thing? Was that thing made of metal? Like an old frying pan? A skillet? Was that rust coming down its sides, like it was crying rust? Why did he feel so attached to it? Why did he feel pulled towards it? Why did it feel like the pull was weakening? Was that his bike-lock? Why couldn't he move his legs? What was that thing blinking on that monitor to his left? Was that a heart monitor? And what was that? A breathing machine? And why was this man so down? Why did he look at him like that? And why was there a piece of thick string attached to his chest, seemingly pulling him towards the door? And why was he refusing? Holding back? Resisting the pull? And the other man too, why did he have the same kind of dark string coming out of his chest? And why did that string, actually more like a chain, hang out the window? A closed window? And what was up with the dark round large object in the corner? Why did it make him feel so down? Why did it make him feel like he knew it? A big ball of iron? One of those that could lazily move through bricks and crush them? Make parts of buildings fall down? A wrecking-ball? A moody wrecking ball? Why was it crying rusty tears? Why couldn't he move his arms? His legs? Why did he feel so light?

This had to be a hospital. But where were his clothes? Was that really snow outside the window? Did he know this person, the sadder of the two? Was that a drip? And was it connected to his arm? He didn't know anyone black. He'd never had a black friend. But this man was crying and holding his hand. And the large friendly ball of metal in the corner was sobbing too. Was he, who just entered, a doctor? Looked like one. Why was he shaking his head? What was that he was holding up? Wolfgang wanted to see too. What was it? Oh, a compass. What did he have a compass for anyway? Was that a form of alternative treatment? He didn't want alternative treatment. Or maybe he actually secretly did? Maybe alternative was what he'd always wanted? But couldn't have? Or be? Why did he think that now? Why did he seem to hear his mother's voice? What was she saying? A compass of love? For Love? Wait. No mum. He thought she was wrong, that was not what this was. Did she see it? Did she see how the needle was all confused and just swirling around? It was like there was no north, no south anymore. Mother? Was she there? He knew, yes, the true compass of love was the love of God, he knew. She'd taught him that a long time ago. And even though he'd made her think he didn't believe her, he'd thought about it, he really had.

Why was the doctor checking that monitor? Why was he holding Wolfgang's wrist? Doctor? Was that really a compass in his hand? Hanging from around his neck in that flimsy red string? Did he just come from some orientation race where one navigates with a map and finds posts in the terrain? Was that why he still had that compass around his neck? He wanted the doctor to please tell him that was the case. To please tell him he'd done well in that race and kind of wanted to show off. He forgave him that. As long as he wasn't administering some kind of alternative treatment. Wolfgang was a scientist. He was a doctor too! Why couldn't he hear him? He wanted to know if that huge sad hunk of iron in the corner was part of the treatment? It rather looked like it needed some help itself. Couldn't he see it? Didn't he just walk right through it? Hey? Didn't he just go over there and look out the window and walk right through that massive sad-looking thing? He wanted to know if he was dreaming? Why was the doctor pointing out the window and describing something he couldn't hear to these black guys? He was getting worried here. He sensed he was ill or something. Was something really wrong with him? This was no ordinary dream, was it? What was that? What did he just try to tell him? Yeah, he was aware the doctor was trying to talk to him. But he wasn't responding, was he? Did the doctor know who he was? Had he found his papers? He wanted the doctor to know he wasn't from around there originally. He was German. His wallet was in his jacket. His driver's license was in his wallet. There was a picture of his ex-girlfriend in there too. He thought she was so beautiful when he first met her. He'd thought about her every day for the last, how many years? Seven? Eight? Since they split. Hey. The big round blobby thing in the corner was crying. Wolfgang asked the big blob if it knew she was OK? Was that a nod? Did the blob nod to him? It felt like it was trying to communicate, by the way it seemed to have a stronger pull on him. She... her name was Jana. Did the blob see his mother just now? Wasn't she the nicest woman? Another nod? Yes, he thought so. He was beginning to like the blob. The huge thing made out of solid metal in the corner there. Wolfgang didn't want it to cry those rusty tears. Would it tell him a story maybe? Did it know stories? Wolfgang said he used to love stories when he was a boy, mostly Bible stories. Did the blob know any Bible stories? No? What about... what about that dream he'd once had when he was... maybe nine? About that bird who slept on his pillow? He had a feeling it must have been there too? Could he tell that one? Did he remember? Yes. That was the one, exactly. He hadn't seen it since – the bird.

Did the ball remember how its wings looked like sort of liquid pulsating fur? Wasn't that beautiful? It had been there, hadn't it? Wolfgang had had a feeling.

Why did they keep looking at the compass? Seemed like north was there one minute, then over there the next? Was that a sigh? Did anybody hear that? Did everything just sigh? Like the whole building and the windows and all of it just sighed? Right? Did it hear it too? God. It felt like, it felt like they were 40,000 years into the past somehow. Something smelled really old, you know, ancient. Prehistoric. Was that possible? For something to be prehistoric? Before history he meant? And smell? Mother? Was she there still? What did the Bible say about that? What about other religions? She didn't know about other religions? OK. Was she leaving? Was that the smell of her perfume? Coco? By Chanel? But she'd been dead for years? Metal-thing? Did it hear her too? Was it? Did the smell of his mother's perfume come through with all that really old smell? Through the walls? From the ground? Why were the walls breathing? Why did everything seem to have life? Was that a flock of birds resting on the windowsill? He guessed they couldn't fly in this weather? Right? That was snow? Right? He felt his large iron friend was tired. Why did large things seem so much sadder when they were sad than small things? Was there simply more sadness to go with more girth? That something really bad must have happened for something so big to be so affected? Was that it? It was making a mess on the floor, by the way, the big thing. There was a whole puddle of dark brown water under it, seeping towards the wall there. It had perhaps better dry that up before it got into the electric system?

Where was Bjørn anyway? And The Dane? Something bad had happened, hadn't it? Big thing? Was it nodding again? Was that a nod? It sure felt like it was nodding to him by the way his chest felt tugged at. Was he connected to it? The big sad iron thing? Somehow? The puddle under it was growing in size. Something would short-circuit. What was the really bad thing that had happened? Doctor? What was the matter? Was he being treated for something serious? And was this, if it was serious, connected to something else? Something outside perhaps? Something to do with why all these birds were sitting at the windowsill? He wasn't in any pain, if that was what he was asking. No. He wasn't. He felt good, as a matter of fact. Only thing was, he couldn't move. But he wasn't panicking. He just felt calm and peaceful. Though he was starting to worry about this huge iron ball the doctor'd just walked straight through again. Something was not right with it. It was crying. The doctor had stepped in its tears just now. He had a feeling something very fundamentally basic had gone totally wrong, flipped or something, lost its way, changed, started a process of alteration, towards something it seemed like no one knew. He got a very basic bad vibe from everyone around him. They all looked downright worried. He'd say they were starting to look spooked. The wrecking-ball too. It looked like it had lost all pep, like it had been paralyzed or something. The doctor had a thick black cord hanging from underneath his white coat. It ran along the floor, before it just went into the wall. Had the doctor given him a drug that made him go on like this? Made him feel happy and talkative? While he could sense all this sadness? And fear? In all of them? He could even sense the birds were anxious. Outside. And when he, when he tried to remember he sensed that, he sensed he just woke up... but was still sleeping. Like his sleep and his dreams had taken over everything. Sad thing with an immense presence, over in the corner, was that it? A tug at his chest again, like the proverbial heartstrings were plucked. But he'd never used that expression before in his life. He didn't even know if he knew the expression. Though he just did. He'd used the expression plucking the heartstrings. Was that because the feeling was exactly like that? Like the feeling could only equal one expression if it was given the right to form itself in words? What metal-blob? Was that it communicating by plucking his heartstrings? And what were heartstrings anyway? He'd never heard of them in any scientific context, though of course they could be a metaphorical way of referring to nerves. What did this thought do in his head? Oh folks, people, cheer up, please, cheer up! They were making him sad here. He wanted them to do something if they were feeling so bad about it, this something they wouldn't let him in on. Did that drip contain a sedative? If so, it was good. He wanted them to have some. They should. The doctor too, yeah him. And wasn't it about time he put away that compass? It was OK. They all got he was a terrific reader of maps, but he was working now. OK?

Wolfgang was tired of this voice. It was going too wild. It didn't let him taste one feeling or emotion before it scooted on. And since when did he talk about tasting feelings? He was an economist damn it! Not a poet. Not an artist. He perhaps thought a lot, and he'd had his downs and lows and... He was alone, no parents left, no sisters, no brothers, no relatives. He suspected that the compass in the doctor's hand was not in any way related to his sports activities, he was getting that feeling now, although he still felt remarkably cheerful. He thought that he'd brought it in to show them, the compass, at least show these two men here by Wolfgang's bed something of significance, and what could that be? Relating to a compass? Had the magnetic poles switched? Had they heard of this phenomenon? How south might become north in just a matter of hours? They knew the theory, right? Magnetic reversal? This drip had some magical qualities. Hey iron-thing, it was bringing him down now, he could feel it, it had a definite effect on him. Were those metal cables? Coming out of Wolfgang's solar plexus? And where did they go? Were they…? Was that the big thing? Were they connected to it? These cables coming out of him? Going over to it? He couldn't feel their weight but they looked damn heavy. Was it pulling at these? Was that what was making him feel melancholic now, underneath this? This patina? Of happiness? Patina? What did that word really mean? He meant, under this, the melancholy he felt coming on, underneath this feeling of calm and quiet brought on by his guess was a morphine-type drug dissolved in that drip? Was the ball responsible for that feeling? By some kind of tugging at the cables? By the way, did it realise it was hovering above ground, Big Thing? Like only a few centimetres? Maybe ten? He definitely felt a vibe from it now, it seemed it was growing in size. If it had shoulders they would be drooping forward, that's how Wolfgang felt about the vibe it was sending. Defeated. Was that right? Was that how it felt? Had it given up on something? Something had given up on it? Somebody? Somebody had let it down, was that it? A nod?

Was that a nod? It felt like a nod. He didn't mean to sound cheerful, like he wasn't taking this seriously. He was. But he felt so relaxed and calm.

Look metal ball, look! The snow had just started falling even heavier. Wasn't that beautiful? Did he fall too? Earlier? He did? Were you? You here on my immediate right here, were you the one who? Were you the one who picked me up?

He was going back now. People! It felt like he was sinking into a darkness. HEY. They were becoming very distant, as if he looked at them through the wrong end of a pair of binoculars. HEY. It was like everything was rushing at him. Things. Moving very fast towards him. He saw… Episodes with a light shimmering behind them. Like they were placed on a light-box. And he was smiling. It felt like he was smiling. Could they see him smile? They couldn't, could they? He was smiling because he was seeing nice things. That was all. Recognising them. Was this the end of his life then? But he'd only lived such a short one? For their times? Could it be? He was getting anxious now. Metal-Ball? Any hints? Was this the end? But he felt so good. So removed. So calm. He wanted to see what was up next. He wanted to find out how things would turn out, change, maybe improve. That was why he'd chosen science in the first place. He always wanted to see what could happen in his lifetime, he meant, in a full lifetime, eighty years or so. So he wasn't going to, was he? Ball? It seemed so impressive and strong. He wished he'd known it earlier. And he wasn't sure he was going to see anyone again, afterwards, like the New Testament said, and his mother had used to. He felt so young. What had happened to him? He was born, grew up, lived a few years, lost his parents, then? It seemed so, it seemed so, like a tease, somehow. Then what? Back to nothingness? Was that what was waiting? Ball of Iron? It seemed so wise. Was that what waited? He felt like the metal-ball had come to keep watch over him. Was it coming too? Or was he following it? Was that a nod again? He thought so. He had a feeling. And these guys here? What about them? And the doctor? Could someone show him the picture in his wallet? The one of Jana? Would someone tell her? He felt like talking to her. She'd been good to him. He hadn't been so good to her, though he'd been for a while, but he'd felt he couldn't stay. It was a long story. What a joke really? If this was it?

Mamma?

/>

/release

Started at Wed Sep 20 02:47:39 27020

Command line was: ./henkick_1266 --out-dir=store/ final_rebuild --out-postfix=arx_run_0_no_clean --creat-sigma=10 --no-plot --save-plot --kwg- base=hk_kwg_9.db --drives-list=drives.txt --drive- idx=105

Version tag 3.12.1.1266, built Wed Sep 20 02:47:36 27020

Job ID is: 214985, 1002 instances allocated

VC hash: f9c8ab31de39

parsing recovered files at /store/recovery/drvB5K

<shovelling_snow

There was a certain rhythm and sound to snow-shovelling
that was quite hypnotic, therapeutic even, when you got
into it, the spade or shovel in your hands, the area covered
in snow in front of you, which it was your responsibility
to clear, at least that day, digging in and heaving back,
digging in and heaving back. You quickly worked up a
sweat and had to open your jacket at the top to let out
some steam. There was a chimney principle to follow to
cool yourself down when you had to wear warm clothes
but still had to work hard. Heat rose upwards. So you
didn't need to take off your jacket completely. It sufficed
to loosen it at the top. And if that wasn't enough, opening
your fly created a draft, the same way you would do with
a wood-burning stove. But you shouldn't take off your hat

unless you absolutely had to, because you lost a lot of heat through your head, maybe too much, too quickly, and with the addition of snow landing in your hair (if you had any) you'd be wet and uncomfortable in a different way than if you'd sweated yourself wet wearing the hat. It was better to dry that hat-sweat away when you were back inside again.

So digging in, finding the rhythm and listening to the sound of the spade or shovel you could feel your body working, getting rid of the toxins, doing what it was meant to do. You felt the weight of the snow at the end of the spade or shovel, you realised you were maybe overdoing the amount you were lifting with each heave, you hit upon some hard icy snow under what looked like a pristine easily fluffed away layer of virgin snow. You fell over, slid, knocked your head on the spade or shovel's handle. You said 'fuck', maybe twice. You got up again, brushed some snow off your trousers and jacket and felt incredibly warm and like saying 'forget it' and going inside, but you waited it out, the anger and the frustration, you let it seep off, you stood still and breathed controlled, the vapour appearing from your mouth like speech-bubbles from cartoon characters, and you heaved to again, and you found the rhythm once more, and you started singing a song to yourself, in your head, the same line of melody over and over, maybe a bit of Springsteen or Chicago, and you started enjoying

the digging in and the throwing behind you again, and
the pavement, if that's where you were, would start to
appear ordered and neat once more, accessible, civilised,
and you'd be happy with yourself and you'd feel physically
well, naturally exhausted. Hungry. At least for a while.

/>

<laughing

Around a large round table at the OXO Tower restaurant (not the brasserie) the core team was tucking into
a supersize casserole of mock bœuf bourguignon. The
beef was substituted with SPAM, the onions with radish-
paste. Instead of actual red wine the sauce was made from
red-wine-powder mixed with Diet Pepsi Cola. It tasted
interesting. They were drinking Really Light Ribena
Raspberry & Pomegranate, the only drink available in
sufficient quantities, as water was strictly rationed and
the Pepsi had been used for the sauce. Bjørn sat next to
his mother, who sat next to the Norwegian Ambassador,
who sat next to Kweku, who sat next to Kirsty, who sat
next to the Mayor, who sat next to the High Commissioner
of Ghana, who sat next to the Norwegian Ambassador's

secretary, who sat next to Bjørn. From their seats they could almost all of them see how the snow fell and settled on the balcony just beyond the glass walls. The rest of the once stunning view was gone in the perpetual whiteness.

The Mayor had expropriated the restaurant just the week before, as no one was using it anyway. They were the only guests. They were cold. It had been a long day at the front of the dumper. Bjørn's mother remembered using OXO bouillon cubes when she was younger. Her mother had used them as well. She listened to the Mayor's meandering story about the conversion of the building from wharf to galleries, offices, apartments and restaurants. She bought his explanation that WHARF was an acronym for Ware-House At River Front. The Ghanaian High Commissioner knew this was wrong, that the word wharf came from the Old English hwearf, meaning "bank" or "shore," but he didn't say anything out of respect for his host. The music played over the loudspeakers embedded in each chair's back-rest was a collection called Rockin' Classics, though not a selection of songs from the 1950s, but up-tempo, rocked-up versions of classical arrangements by Beethoven, Mozart, Hayden, Vivaldi; a walking base line and some rock percussion added to the bottom of The Four Seasons; an electric guitar playing the theme of Für Elise, and so on. They could none of them figure out where the infernal speakers were placed. The Mayor was humming along between talking and chewing and checking his phone. The falling snow made the secretary to the Norwegian Ambassador seasick, at least that's what she said she was. She couldn't stand the continuous downwards movement of so many large particles.

Bjørn wasn't listening as he was trying to catch Kirsty's eyes, desperately, his mother thought. He would never attract her that way. A man needed to neglect a woman to receive her attention. That was the commonly agreed rule of courtship, a rule Bjørn knew, but had started thinking was ridiculous, as a man could only ignore a woman if he really didn't like her, in which case there was no reason for him to try to get her attention in the first place.

The Norwegian Ambassador was stuffing SPAM into his napkin. His secretary was falling asleep. Kweku was expanding his theory of magnets to Kirsty, telling her how they now, most likely all of them present, had magnets right now, out there, whose paths formed an intricate mesh or web, that they now, as people, most likely held each other in place, by sitting as they were, around a circular table. Kirsty nodded and thought it made sense. It was a simple powerful theory the more she felt she understood it. She knew what Kweku meant when he said that people always felt pulled somewhere. Energy, Kweku told her, was all there was. That energy was a closed system. How nothing got lost. How a pull here lead to a stumble there, the stumble leading to a knock on the head, as had happened to Wolfgang. How this could have terrible consequences as they'd seen. Where was Wolfgang's magnet now? Kirsty wanted to know. Kweku said he wasn't sure, but that it had to be somewhere. Kirsty nodded, but the thought made her worried. She stared at her glass of Ribena. If Kweku didn't know where magnets went when people died, then that was something she couldn't live with, at least if she was going to accept his theory. Either the magnet had taken Wolfgang with him, or? But on a planet with so many people dying and being born every day, was there space for so many outmoded magnets? So many rusty entities just hanging about? Left to slowly disintegrate in a separate dimension? Kweku felt he couldn't explain his theory well enough. This made him worried he didn't really know what he was talking about. Maybe it was just bullocks? He'd never seen the magnet. Was the magnet theory just a parable? A way of saying that things were connected? That a certain mass had a certain effect on another?

They were all around the table freezing terribly, almost shaking from freezing so much, when all of a sudden the music coming from the chairs disappeared. This made them stop talking. They stopped eating too and put down their cutlery and looked at each other. They could hear the sound of their blood pumping in their heads. Their eyes passed from one to another. They couldn't hold anyone's gaze, but kept looking from face to face around the table. They smiled and nodded. No one felt they could look down, nor keep their head still. The Norwegian Ambassador's right eye went into a spasm, winking mechanically. His stiff smile was moments from bursting his upper lip, just under his nose. His secretary threw up in her mouth and swallowed again. The Ambassador dropped his SPAM-packed napkin on the floor and laughed out loud. The Ghanaian High Commissioner politely joined with a hearty laugh. So did Liv, first quietly, then roaringly, and more and more desperately, going purple in the cheeks, tears spouting from her eyes. The Mayor couldn't hold back either, seeing this, and rumbled into a prolonged set of his loudest HA HAs. They all laughed, madly, supposedly life-savingly, for minutes, and none of them had any idea why.

Then The Magic Flute overture came back through the speakers again, featuring a slap bass and a bossa nova rhythm section, and everyone sighed with relief, dried their eyes and looked down at their plates.

/>

<eyes

Kirsty went out on the balcony for one of her last real cigarettes. Kweku followed her. There was some shelter from the snow on the eastern side of the building, under an awning extending a few metres. Standing so high up, looking into the falling snow, was nauseating. Flakes whirled, fell denser, then a bit lighter, then denser, then very much denser, then lighter again, like a restless personality wanting something, something it didn't really know what. They'd left their coats inside. Behind the tall glass windows their table was being cleared. Kweku asked for a cigarette. Kirsty trembled handing it to him, lighting it. He inhaled, coughed and felt instantly dizzy. He'd never smoked before. He felt his blood vessels contracting in a radial wave out from his chest into his fingers, down into his toes. They both still hummed along silently to the infernal dinner-muzak. Kirsty sought out Kweku's eyes, looked into their whiteness and darkness, high-contrasted by his black skin and hair, the whirling snow behind his head. He didn't mind. He let her do it. It made her feel odd. What was going on here? She felt she saw something heavy in each of them, like an iron mass, shining, polished, a great force inert, waiting patiently, idling like a powerful engine would. It felt like these masses pulled her into his head. She thought she saw them pulling away, receding fast; that she went with them. To either side she felt she saw intense sunlight, then a red dirt road, then a stretch of scattered palm trees, a field littered with old punctured footballs, and beyond, behind, was the sense of a large cloud of dust kicked up, a thundering herd of buffalos running through it. It felt like the iron balls were waiting on the other side of the cloud, giving her time to catch up. It felt like she saw the origins of a smile, no, make that many smiles, very old ones, then multiple beginnings of belly-laughs. The smiles' and the laughs' compounded energy was undulating, still and powerful, just for her. Fighting his dizziness Kweku saw how Kirsty's pupils dilated, how they looked like something someone might fall into and never emerge from. Her Aegean-green irises were turbulent storms of stringy gasses around this twin central darkness.

He saw his own reflection in the corneas, his own eyes like double light-sources falling into the dark holes behind. He blinked and felt like the green storm either side of her eyes' darkness buzzed and fizzed. He felt the instant appearance of a boner down his suit pants. He arched his lower back to avoid tentage. He felt his face going warm, like a mug filling up from the neck upwards, like each individual hair on his head were given a name and an address. He felt ashamed, awkward really, because: what he saw in there, what he saw in her eyes, what was pulling him in, was so honest, so terribly young. Five-year-old Kirsty pedalling away on a rusty tri-cycle. The same young Kirsty washing an apple in a puddle of mud. So innocent. Early teenage Kirsty getting her first period in gym-class. Mid-teenage Kirsty discovering she actually liked peas, and fish, even olives. Kirsty the lanky beauty-bud, pushing eighteen, really uncomfortable in everyone's company, her own included. Far in there, far into the darkness of her dilating pupils, hiding from eyes that weren't even looking. It was awkward, Kweku felt, how the electric iris-green all around this hidden innocence connected so powerfully and directly with his penis. Confusing really. Contradictory. How was this green so wise? How could this colour know what it wanted? And make him aware of what he wanted too? Erudite Green? Was that its name? Did his penis prefer this colour? And could eyeballs be tugged at? It certainly felt like it. Kirsty sensed the double iron masses in Kweku's eyes readying to go further in, looking at their watches and hiking double thumbs over their shoulders. The cloud of buffalo-dust was slowly settling before them. Were they putting on sunglasses? It felt like they throttled their engines. Was that moisture down below? That slightly viscous feeling between her upper thighs? No man had handed his eyes to her like this before. Never. No man had ever stared back for this long. Kweku's erection was throbbing like a sore thumb behind his thin trousers, the Marks & Spencer jockeys, impatient, needy. He felt he was sucked closer, further, into the expanding darkness at the centre of each of Kirsty's eyeballs. He couldn't see his own reflections anymore, only the shadows of the falling snowflakes at the edges. He saw into her past, it was obvious. It lived in there, caught by the dark material, the things she'd seen, absorbed into the vitreous humour and locked away. Kirsty felt she experienced the round metal masses turning around, inside Kweku's head, then speeding off, pulling her with them, further in, past actual and metaphorical mountains of bullshit, through a dank and dark college office, into an airplane, down underground in a tube-train, through streets at dusk, into a cathedral. And her nose touched Kweku's. She closed her eyes. Kweku felt the icy nose on his warm and shameful one. He shut his eyes too. He kept his lower back arched, extending his bum like a speed-reducing device, his member cowering moray eel-style. And the powerful pull of his desire was fun, and the counterpart he felt in Kirsty, its excitement, its surprised quality, was really fun too, and not at all what he'd dreamt of – no, never. But no doubt what he'd wanted, now that it was there, so close, so magnetic, so in his face. So they kissed a while, as the snow fell densely, totally disinterested in the trajectory of their lives. Behind them.

/>

<delegation_party_time

The snow-removal delegation party had moved from the OXO Tower restaurant (not the brasserie) over to the OXO Tower bar for post-dinner drinks and relaxation, karaoke and small-talk, and perhaps even some dancing. The bar was closed to the public, but the delegation counted a good modern air-conditioned bus-load by this stage, so there wasn't really a feeling of being in a poorly attended bar in a once-every-thirty-thousand-years-snow-storm, though it was obviously snowing outside the large floor-to-ceiling windows surrounding the bar on the 8th floor, snowing as if someone had ordered the party-variety-act-version of snowing, that is, it was snowing with an over-the-top kind of exhilarating kitschy quality. Everyone was happy that the infernal sourceless music from the restaurant had been replaced by a very mediocre house band. The organic sound of actual drums and piano and standing bass felt sexy, dry-humpy, and was the probable cause of much of the obscene lustfulness on view. The barmen were shaking very large quantities of vodka-martinis in improvised cut-in-half and smacked-together-again two-litre plastic-bottles of Pepsi. The delegation members associated prohibition-era extravagant party-images from films they'd seen as they laughed and winked, full of abandonment, cheekiness and verve and plain old-fashioned pre-snow fun, spurred on by the fact that this was the first real party they'd been to in weeks, no, make that months.

From his perched barstool position Bjørn could see that his mother was already dancing with the Mayor. Of all the people in the bar Bjørn was the least in classic party-mood. He was observing Kirsty dancing with Kweku, dancing in that timeless way that didn't spell restraint; a mix between a Lambada, a Tango and a Shiatsu-massage. He thought about the cliché he'd heard a trillion times, the one about black men and their quality of endowment. It hurt him very personally to think about this. Not that he was a racist, far from it, but the imagined hurtful image in his mind was nonetheless on a par with what he thought of as an image of his private sense of self being eaten alive by a white shark in a misty morning scene. Kweku was a very good dancer. Bjørn couldn't deny that. He looked olympian as he plastered Kirsty to his torso and led her confidently in-between the pudding-clutches of the other dancers. His mother and the Mayor seemed like a pair of time-and-memory-challenged toads in comparison. Also, Kweku was one of the genuinely nicest guys he'd ever met, and Bjørn wasn't overcompensating for his fear of being a racist when he thought that. This man was the closest Bjørn had ever been to meeting a reward-card kind of man. The kind that wasn't just happy and good-looking and smart, but understanding and witty and ironic (at the right time, in right doses), who also happened to stand a good head taller than himself. Bjørn felt he had plenty of good reasons for being down if the attention Kirsty was paying Kweku was in any way indicative of her feelings as spectacular-woman looking for a man to have fun with, perhaps even start a meaningful relationship with.

He knocked back his dirty martini and indicated a refill to the closest barman. He saw his mother whispering something into the Mayor's right ear as they slowly trudged around the other dust-shufflers on the improvised dance floor. He saw the Mayor laugh. His mother liked dancing. It gave her face a happy sort of stupid expression, like she wouldn't hear you if you went up to her and said something easily understood. He remembered seeing photos of his father and mother dancing, the same lameish expression on her face. It was mostly a happy expression though, its silly quality provided by a sense of childishness, of being secure in a big man's arms. She had a weakness for big and tall men. Her father had been one.

Kweku lifted Kirsty up and spun her one full rotation in the air. She screamed and looked delighted. Bjørn's refill came. He emptied it in one gulp, olive included, and indicated one more. He could sense the shape of his hangover already. It felt like it was sitting next to him, an old brown-toothed hangover, ogling him and squeezing its hands for every drink he murdered. The band was playing a jazzy version of Here Comes Santa Claus. What month was it anyway? Several of the delegation's army officers had taken off their jackets and were swinging them above their heads, down by the corner-table facing the west and the river. It looked like they tried to helicopter, like small boys thinking they could levitate if they only swung the jackets fast enough. Bjørn laughed a short derisive laugh and shook his head. Santa had stopped arriving and the band announced a twenty-minute break. He was happy to see his mother let go of the Mayor and head for the toilets. The Mayor looked lonely without her, on the emptying dance floor, not sure what to do with himself. He seemed vaguely Parkinsonistic, aflutter somehow, as if his large frame and big head were empty and breeze-sensitive. Maybe it was the delayed air-current from the swinging officer's jackets that had hit him? A hand was put on Bjørn's shoulder. He turned around and saw that it belonged to Kirsty. She was smiling at him. He could see she was warm from the dance with Kweku. He couldn't see Kweku. He tried to smile, but felt too slighted to really make it.

"Can I sit down?"

"Of course."

She jumped up on the bar-stool next to Bjørn's. Her shoulders were bare. She'd cut her hair short, sort of, probably because of having to wear a hat all day.

"And Kweku?"

"Had to leave. Major dumper crash over by Buckingham Palace. Three or four vehicles apparently. The scout just came with the message."

"Really? That's bad. So he had to go?"

"Yeah. Annoying, at this time of night. And you? How are you doing?"

"Ah, you know me, you know. Not much of a dancer."

"I didn't know that. Don't think I've ever seen you dance. Is it that bad?"

"It's bad, trust me."

She was smiling at him.

"Your mother seems to enjoy it?"

"Yeah, don't ask. It's... she's always liked to dance."

He felt he was slurring his words, that he was leaning too much forward.

"And you Kirsty?"

"You mean dancing?"

"Yeah, and... in general?"

"I really like to dance. Kweku's an amazing dancer, don't you think? So with him it's easy. Did you see how he threw me up in the air?"

"No. Sounds. Exciting."

He tried to get the attention of the barman to order another martini. He wasn't looking at Kirsty. They didn't say anything for a while. The sound of the chatter around them was intense. Bjørn felt extremely drunk. He closed his eyes.

He woke to again as he felt Kirsty's hand on his upper arm.

"Oh," he said. He tried to look her in the eyes, blinking slowly. Then he asked her if she was OK, but she didn't answer that, or at least he thought he'd asked her that and that she hadn't answered.

"Do you remember what you told me once?"

Her voice was faint in among the clatter of glasses and the shaking of martinis. He closed his eyes and felt himself swaying, that the only secure thing in his world at that moment was the feeling of her hand on his upper arm.

"I don't know. I guess not. When?"

"When we were in Greenland."

"No. I don't remember."

His head did a downwards drop and swing and came up right-side looking at Kirsty. He smiled drunkenly, his eyes red and moist. He felt angry with her, angry with himself for being angry and drunk and feeling cynical and careless and sorry for himself.

"Were you there? I mean. Did you also come to Greenland?"

"Is that a joke?"

Her hand dropped from his shoulder.

"I don't know. Tell me."

"Tell you what?"

"I don't know, something. What's Kweku like?"

"Kweku?"

"Yes."

Bjørn felt he was about to fall off the stool, that the room was spinning him around. He noticed Kirsty was looking the other way. Then she turned to him again.

"You're drunk Bjørn. Kweku has nothing to do with it. At least he didn't. Not until tonight."

Her voice was colder. Not rude. Just differently pitched, in a sad disappointed way. He didn't reply. He couldn't reply if he'd wanted to, which he did. He wanted her to like him, to see that he'd always liked her. His head fell forward then bobbed up again a few times.

"You told me you'd look me in the eyes. When we spoke on the phone, from each our room. You told me you'd look me in the eyes, the next time you saw me. But you don't remember...?"

She slid off her stool and stood still for a moment, her arms hanging childlike by her sides.

Bjørn smiled with only half his face, one eye closed, trying to focus on one of her. He wanted to tell her that he'd loved her for a long long time. But he wasn't able to. His self-pity and pride and the alcohol in his head didn't allow him. He made out that she was turning around to go. As she was walking away he wanted to call her name to make her come back, but said:

"I don't care anymore."

Or at least he thought he said it.

/>

/love

Started at Thu Sep 21 01:26:08 27020

Command line was: ./henkick_1267 --out-dir=store/
final_rebuild --out-postfix=arx_run_0_no_clean
--creat-sigma=10 --no-plot --save-plot --kwg-
base=hk_kwg_9.db --drives-list=drives.txt --drive-
idx=106

Version tag 3.12.1.1267, built Thu Sep 21 01:26:05
27020

Job ID is: 166729, 1048 instances allocated

VC hash: 1af76f26a2de

parsing recovered files at /store/recovery/drvT3N

＜up_in_the_air

In the snow that was not only coming down over the UK, but right across the whole of Northern Europe, the Dane's mother's grave was completely covering over.

According to the report filed by the night shift doctor, she was found dead by the team of paramedics sent out to answer the distress-call. It had been a distress-call from a certified county medical authority personal alarm given to elderly people suffering from a serious disease but not ill enough to be in an institution permanently. The Dane's mother had had the alarm for well over three years before her death and had used it twice before. On these previous occasions she'd been resuscitated using electro-shock, which had given her broken ribs and caused her a lot of subsequent pain when breathing and coughing. She smoked a lot so she coughed a lot. She was one of the youngest in the history of the county to have been granted the alarm. According to the report there'd been no attempt at resuscitation on the night of her death. She'd been dead for a while when the paramedics arrived. The report concluded that the cause of death was heart failure as a consequence of a severe asthmatic attack. It did not mention that she'd been an alcoholic, going in and out of institutions for the last fifteen years. But her considerable medical journal gave evidence to this fact. Her journal was towards the end of her life made fully electronic and was kept in copy, according to Danish law, for potential future statistical purposes, stored in a so-called cloud-computing facility in the Republic of Ireland, governed by several EU laws for data protection.

In any case, data was just a sequence of Os and 1s. No one knew or had decided how long such data should be kept or how long it was realistic to imagine it would stay intact. Those who worked with computers both from a hardware and software perspective knew there was a lot most people weren't told about how computers worked, that they could be as fickle and unpredictable as almost anything. That is: prone to unexpected failure.

What the electronic medical report filed by the night-shift doctor did not include was that the Dane's mother had not eaten anything for a week prior to her death. It did not mention that her flat, provided to her by the county, had not been cleaned since the day she'd moved in three years prior. It did not mention the piles of newspapers in every room, the stacks of crime-fiction paperbacks, all the empty vodka bottles and beer cans.

Her daughter had been notified of her mother's death in the morning, as she was the only next of kin mentioned in the journal. She had then tried to call the Dane on a number he had once provided, but had only heard a recorded English voice saying that the number was no longer in use. She had sent him an email he'd read later in the day. The funeral took place on a Thursday morning. It was mid-summer – mild, but a little rainy. The Dane's sister had insisted he should attend. And out of a sense of loyalty to her he'd made the journey from London on a cheap flight, due to go back in the evening. The coffin was light and small, almost the size of coffins made for children. She had shrunk considerably during her last years.

The incident report did not mention that she'd been found on the floor among the piles of newspapers, head down, nose broken. It had estimated the time of death to somewhere between 01.50 a.m. when the call had been registered, and 02.20 a.m. when the paramedics had found her after spending some time forcing down the solid front door she'd always kept double-locked.

Her grave was in the town of Holstebro, Jutland. It was a very modest grave. The stone was grey speckled granite, only polished on the side where her name and dates were inscribed in gold letters and numbers. The inscription under her name and dates read, in Danish: Takk for alt, which meant Thanks for everything or Thank you for everything, depending on how strict your translation was. The stone was otherwise left untreated, to give an impression of being a stone, one would presume, and old, and rugged, where moss could gather more easily. It was a stone similar to other stones in that area of the graveyard, but unlike stones of eras gone by that were placed in other parts. Even gravestones followed fashions.

A few birch trees planted in that part of the cemetery ten years before she died had not really grown to be very tall, and in winter none of them could be said to be impressive, so directly above her grave there was just the open sky. It was the Dane's sister who'd arranged the stone, and the funeral, though the Dane had been there. He just hadn't participated much in the practical side of it.

In summer the view from where her stone was placed was quite pleasant towards the east, across a little artificial lake into a row of taller elms in the distance. These trees moved beautifully in summer breezes. Not that very many ever noticed this fact. Just that the Dane remembered it

now and then when he thought of his mother's funeral.
He hadn't been back there since. He sometimes wondered
where he would be buried. There was no place that singled
itself out yet, but time would surely tell, he thought, and
tried to think of something else.

/>

<making_love

When he was fucking Alice, resting on both arms, like doing push-ups, the Dane's mind would usually fill up with images of women in porn-videos. He would see a series of heavily made up eyes that were supposed to look seducing, he would hear the slapping of arse-cheeks. He would hear the fuck me fuck me fuck me cries of women in porn-videos. He would see legs and arses and pussies in a maelstrom of different coloured flesh, a kaleidoscopic vortex of body parts that entered into orifices and got pulled out again before being put back in again, endlessly, with the fuck me fuck me fuck me soundtrack interspersed with his own inner voice going, as if he was Alice, pull down my panties, pull down my panties, pull down my panties, with a third section of the score being Alice's soft moans below him, actually far below him due to their difference in height, her eyes staring right into his chest between his nipples. He felt himself slacken immediately. He pulled out. She would not move, not say anything. He sat up, rested on his knees, his head hanging down, his forehead and hair sweaty. His penis continuing to shrink rapidly, like a creature on a coral reef sensing danger. The porn-video-brain-cloud would continue to play out on a slow fade to static for about 30 seconds. Thighs and tits and latex and nylon and stilettos and pricks and fannies and overly lit couches and potbellied tattooed hunks and sundrenched pools and baby oil and no pubic hair whatsoever and sad expressions and hurting expressions and humiliated expressions and animalistic pain reactions and shockingly arousing situations involving many men and a few girls or many girls and the one lucky guy and machines that were straddled by "teenage" girls and two "lesbians" mud-wresting, all of it played out in his head in the cloud of porn-noise for a good 30 seconds while he hung his head and his penis went puppy limp, until he heard and thought nothing, absolutely nothing, but felt an all-consuming shame, as in, he would like to be anywhere but right there and then feeling so self-consciously naked and unprotected. That was when Alice touched his forehead, brushing his sweaty hair aside and pulled him down towards her again and kissed him with a wet tongue and his shame evaporated and his penis appeared hard and fully erect again, like a ghost, and she took hold of it and directed it into herself and for a few moments the Dane was released from himself, utterly, feeling the proverbial stupidness that fucking was supposed to bring on, the emptiness of mind. For a few moments in the missionary position he did not exist as him, he was free, his nose buried in her hair. But before long his brain was brought back online again, with a single very arousing and at the same very disturbing thought about Alice and his sexual appetite for her: that she was only nineteen! That he was having sex with a much younger girl. That she was allowing him to fuck her. This was the thought that made him come, feeling immediately shameful again. He let himself fall halfway onto the mattress and halfway on top of her, caressing her side with one hand, feeling very depressed and thinking that it would've been much better for all involved if he'd never been born, remembering how, in her drunkenness, his mother had once asked him if he'd like to try it with her, feeling endlessly brought down by the thought of all the time between now and his death, all the living he still had to do, all the energy and courage it took to even bother doing the smallest thing, all the self-control needed, all the restraint and all the trivial interactions he would have to have with people he didn't know, didn't

even want to start thinking about getting to know, his
nose still buried in her nice-smelling hair, the very real
person lying next to him, with her own hopes and fears,
lying half-way under him, saying nothing, only breathing.
/>

<forgetting

The key to the cell turned and the heavy door opened with the sound of something vacuum-packed gasping for air. The Dane opened his eyes. He was shaking though he wasn't cold, at least he didn't feel cold. The light in the cell was provided by a solitary bulb somewhere high up. There was also what looked like one half of a dog's food-tray up there, reflecting the naked cell, protecting a CCTV camera. The Dane was shaking from somewhere inside that felt intolerant to the air in the cell, the cold white tiles, the open metallic toilet.

"Hi," said a voice.

The Dane blinked, wondering if his headache was visible from the outside, as in, whether his head was pulsating visibly, like a really sore thumb. He put his tongue in the way of his clattering teeth to see if a different pain would take away the other one. Be more tolerable.

"I'm the duty therapist. This is the police doctor," the voice said.

There was no way the pain of biting his tongue could compete with the headache. The Dane blinked again and swallowed the blood. He was positive the thumping inside his head was audible outside it.

Someone covered him with a blanket. Someone took hold of his wrist and held it for a while. The light in the room felt ferocious, colder than liquid methane, immobilising. Something was wrapped tight around his upper arm, then tighter, then tighter, tighter. Until it exhaled.

"His blood pressure's low. Pulse regular though."

"OK."

"You want him under observation? Heart monitor?"

"No. Think he'll be fine. Needs a drip. A sedative. Will you be here for a while?"

"Sure."

The voice that spoke last was female.

"Can you hear me?" it spoke again.

The Dane blinked. His eyes watered. The presumed owner of the voice bent over him, found his arms under the blanket and started rubbing them up and down.

"Did you see the snow? Incredible, isn't it?"

Her voice was pitched just right so close to his ear. The weight of her leaning chest was too heavy. The rubbing felt good. She smelled nice. He blinked again and a few tears fell down his cheeks. He kept his eyes closed but couldn't find the darkness he needed. His eyelids fired bursts like rocket launches for every heartbeat that went through them. A circular standing wave of light flushed back and forth between each thump.

"OK. Here we go."

The second voice returned. The first voice stopped rubbing his arms. He thought he let out a loud moan. Then he felt a weird nauseating feeling in his right arm and the headache drifted into the horizon, a crisp cool digital blue and simultaneously warm, flesh-coloured horizon. He relaxed and stopped shaking.

"I'll be here when you wake up," the first voice said.

He sat on a beach and heard the sound of the surf. His mother and father and uncles and aunts and sister sat next to him. It felt like they were waiting for him to do something. The pebbles in the surf clunked meaningfully. What they said was: snow, then: art, then: food, then: football. His mother's brother held up a gold watch for him to admire. Over the horizon a large TV-screen showed all kinds of sports at the same time. He said "swell" in an American accent to his uncle's expectant face, though he knew he was Danish. The beach was crawling with sand fleas shooting off at crazy angles. His mother was undressing. He tried to ignore this fact. She ran naked, her flesh bobbing, into the sea and swam away. He shouted that she should come back. A dog was rubbing up against his side. It felt like the dog was the reason there were so many fleas on the beach, though he knew this was wrong. He noticed that his mother had returned, still naked, a female version of the Michelin man, that she was looking at him together with the rest of his family. They were all naked. He told them he was moving home. They laughed, then pointed to a giant turtle coming slowly up the beach, headed straight for the Dane. He was happy to see it. It told him that sea lions were in charge under water. That seemed right. He saw his family walking off down the endless twilighted beach, into a dark blue and pink orange sunset, under the giant TV screen, a zapping sound in the background. He wanted to run after them but was unable to. He ate an entire cheeseburger in one bite, three small bags of prawn-cocktail crisps, then felt like the beach was turning on its side. This was making him anxious. A woman without a face presented her breasts to him and he buried his face in their doughiness. It felt like she started sucking him off too. It felt good but watery, like she was sucking with an ocean inside her mouth.

"How are you feeling?"

He awoke slowly. The first voice looked at him. It belonged to a woman in her late forties was the Dane's guess. She had dark short hair. Wrinkles around her mouth like someone had tied it too tight. The beginnings of cancerous freckles like ice-floats around her temples. She wore glasses that didn't make too much of a statement. Some discreet lipstick and a bit of rouge. He was no longer in the cell but lying on a hard institutional sofa in a strip-lit office. There was a window with snow falling behind it.

"Slept well?"

"Yes."

"Headache?"

"No."

"Wondering where you are?"

"Yes."

"Not to worry. Albany Street police station. But you're not under arrest. Not anymore."

The Dane felt a cold kind of panic take hold and bolted upright, which was a bad idea as the clinically lit room started bobbing up and down around him, ducking and diving, aiming to give him a punch. The chair came at him first. Got him on the nose. The pain blanked his mind.

"Take it easy."

He slumped back onto the hard sofa, holding its edge to make it lie down, trying to escape the bright strip-light. His nose started giving up some easily flowing liquid.

"We gave you a strong painkiller. You've slept for five hours."

The furniture seemed to settle down, the angry chair pulled back into its corner. There was definitely blood coming out of the Dane's nose, seeping down his throat. He was given the voice's perfumed hanky. Its cleanness and softness calmed him. Reminded him of his long dead grandmother.

"You don't have to stay, but you might want to just have a chat. You said some pretty disturbing things last night. Do you remember what happened? We know now you didn't light that fire."

"Fire?"

"Yes, the police found you in an office with the sprinklers running full blast."

The Dane couldn't remember.

"What's the last thing you remember?"

"Leaving my apartment. Going to see my girlfriend. Then on the bus."

"Did you take the tube?"

"Don't remember. I normally do, to see her. Does she know I'm here?"

"Someone here spoke to someone called Bjørn last night."

"And?"

"Snow has cut off the phones by now, so no, we don't know."

Snow? He felt the cold panic rising again, ready to hit him in the guts this time. The flakes were coming down peacefully outside the window.

"It's OK. You can go to her when you're feeling better. Just take it easy for now. She'll be fine, as long as you're fine."

Her kind voice made him relax. She felt so honest and decent. So solid. He was sorry he was ruining her hanky.

"If you want to, you can talk to me about it. Anything you feel like saying is OK. Understood? I'm a therapist. It stays with me."

She was right. There was something. Something he needed to talk about. He knew he would have to change. That it would kill him to keep living the way he'd been going. He wanted to be a better boyfriend. A better brother. Knew he'd been given a new lease somehow, deservedly or not. He was alive, barely so, but still. Alive. Something must have popped in him. He felt so different. Somewhere significant inside, something must have given. Maybe some major bubble had burst? In his sleep? In his drunken coma? Some greasy plug pulled that had held him up?

Stopped the shit from draining? And now it was gone? It felt possible. Even though he was dizzier than a bee in a punchbowl. Or was it just a drunkard's moment of clarity? He knew he needed to talk about it, sooner or later – that talking would be good.

"I don't know where to start," he said and began to cry.

"That's OK," she said and got up from her desk and walked over to the sofa.

"How about your mother? You called for her all night."

She sat down by his feet.

"Is that where it usually starts?"

"It's not a bad place to begin, no. In your case I'd say it's perhaps overdue?"

She was dead-on of course. Maybe the obviousness of what had been bugging him had made it invisible? His fear of being a cliché? Of being fucked by an unhappy childhood? A mother issue?

"I don't…"

He closed his eyes and felt as lonely as he'd ever felt. He felt he didn't belong anywhere. Like everywhere he'd ever been had closed up, the people gone home, the shop sold. He turned on his side and pulled his long legs up to his chest and hugged them. He visualised his childhood room, its blue paint, the heavy TV next to the window. He saw the long acres of newly ploughed farmland past the apple tree, a distant tractor moving slowly along and the black crows behind it. The wide-open sky over the landscape to the north. The v-shaped formations of trekking birds, high up. He heard the sound of the swallows crawling back into their nest under the roof above his window. He thought about his unfinished thesis in comparative lit. His months in hospital after his last breakdown. His mother's grave and the trees next to it. Her deteriorating alcoholism. The heaps of newspapers in her apartment. The dust shovelled into adjacent piles. The stacks of yellowing crime novels by her sofa. The men who'd beat her, while he was sleeping in his room, upstairs. The things she'd said to him when she'd been drunk. The unbelievable shame of it. That he still missed her terribly. The thousands of hours of TV he'd watched. His ambitions to be an artist. The pointlessness of wanting to be an artist when it couldn't support him. His total lack of any kind of income at all. The unspeakable debt he'd accumulated with the bank.

"Let's try something simpler perhaps. Why do you think you're here? Basically?"

He opened his eyes and looked at this woman whose job it was to make him feel better, at least good enough to go back to his rented room. The faint shadows of the falling snowflakes outside the window moved down her face as if her freckles had come alive and wanted to escape the cold light in the ceiling.

"Why aren't you at your girlfriend's?

"..."

"Why do you think you got so drunk?"

He knew the therapist's soft skin was due to the daily application of moisturiser.

"I wanted to..." he started but couldn't get further.

She put her bony hands on his lower legs, took hold of his socked feet and started rubbing them expertly. It felt soothing. A bit too intimate.

"Do you want another painkiller? I'm not supposed to give you any more, but I'm not sure you're quite ready to talk yet."

He nodded and started crying again. She was right. He wanted to talk but couldn't. She got up and brought back a tin-foil sheet of ten 500mg co-codamols from her bag. He popped two with some water and lay back down.

"These are my own, so don't mention it to the doctor if he asks."

She took two herself, turned off the strip-light and sat down in the sofa, putting the Dane's legs and feet back in her lap.

"Don't worry," she said. "Let's just sleep. I've been working a double-shift myself."

The Dane looked out the window, the snowfall more intense now that the room was dark. He felt better. Then he felt he started drifting off into sleep, which made him afraid he wasn't going to be able to wake up again, but he couldn't find the strength to get up, and the drifting felt so seductive, the hypnotic snowfall so cosy.

He sailed off on an inflatable pool float. The water under him was turquoise, endlessly deep. It was death. The beach was always within reach; if he wanted to he knew he could paddle himself in. But he kept drifting across the blue ocean, the yellow pool float making squeaky noises when he shifted about. All kinds of creatures were swimming in the deep. They didn't come up to the surface. He knew their shapes and sizes. Many of them were hideous. Frightening. Some were beautiful. Elegant. Moved with a lot of speed and agility. He knew if he drifted further out he would be gone. There was a break out there. He could hear the roar of the wave across the sub-surface mountain. He turned on his back and looked up. Far above him stars were falling, slowly, eternally, both towards and away from him. He smiled. His smile warmed him to his core, to where it felt like his soul sat perched on a ladder in his chest. His soul held its head in its hands, lost in thought. The ladder the soul was sitting on was a lightweight aluminium extendable one. He asked his soul if it was sad? It said it was. He wanted to ask it why, but was unable to. What he said instead was that he'd just seen something beautiful. This made the soul smile. Then his soul pointed to another soul. This was his mother's soul. The Dane looked at his mother's soul, smiling at it. He said he was happy to meet it. It said it was happy to meet him too. This soul sat in a cold Teflon frying pan. The Dane started crying and the ocean lifted his pool float up to the falling stars and he grabbed hold of one and fell away from the earth, from the pool float, further and further, till he was gone.

He jerked himself into a sitting position, gasping for air. It was daylight in the office. The therapist was gone. Outside the window the snow was falling densely still. He got to his feet and saw a note on the desk: *Take the boots and the jacket by the door. There are more painkillers in the pocket.* ☺ *Florence*

He got dressed. Left the police station without being noticed. There didn't seem to be anyone around. He walked in the heavy snow all the way through North London, the boots a little too tight, the jacket a bit short in the back, past the growing crowds that were looting the high streets, the hundreds of cars already on fire, smouldering, smoking into the snowdrift, to Alice's apartment. He knocked on her door. She opened and hugged him and let him in.

"I think I've got something to tell you," he said.

"I'm so glad you're here," she answered.

He took off his new boots, hung up his new jacket and together they walked into her living room and sat down on her messy bed and started talking.

By then he'd forgotten his dreams that night, his visions, his hallucinations. He'd almost even forgotten Florence the therapist. He remembered nothing of his ordeal in the tube underground, nothing of his drunken wanderings down Camden High Street, the fall he'd had by Euston station. He'd forgotten the monumental headache he'd suffered in the police cell, how cold he'd been, the painful light in the ceiling, the kind foot-rub he'd been given. But he knew he wanted to do things differently. That he wanted something else. He just had to find the right words for it.

/>

/freezing

Started at Fri Sep 22 03:13:53 27020

Command line was: ./henkick_1268 --out-dir=store/final_rebuild --out-postfix=arx_run_0_no_clean --creat-sigma=10 --no-plot --save-plot --kwg-base=hk_kwg_9.db --drives-list=drives.txt --drive-idx=107

Version tag 3.12.1.1268, built Fri Sep 22 03:13:50 27020

Job ID is: 438151, 1558 instances allocated

VC hash: 9d6fa3ce845f

parsing recovered files at /store/recovery/drvI2D

<the_hug

Bjørn's mother was sitting at the rickety IKEA table, drinking whisky. Bjørn had got himself a glass too and was sipping what really wasn't whisky but whisky-essence and moonshine. It had been a long day's work for both. Snow had been cleared, but more snow had been falling, on top of the old, non-stop. Apart from the whistling of the wind outside it was quiet in the room. The dishwasher hadn't run for months, the neighbours had almost all disappeared, no planes were heard bruising the sky, the snow muffled the usual outdoor sounds. Bjørn thought it smelled dusty and stale.

"Look at it," Liv said, pointing at the falling, whirling snow past the floor-to-ceiling windows.

"How long have I been here now?"

"I don't know. Eight months? I've lost track. What month is it now anyway?"

"I don't know either. June? Maybe eight months. It feels longer. Feels like I've been here for years."

She shook her head. Bjørn thought the smell in the room had to be bad for your sinuses. The dryness.

They both stared hypnotised out the window for a while. The snow lay heavy against it. Just a metre of the outside world was visible towards the top, like they were looking out a hole cut into the roof of an igloo.

"How do you feel mamma? Your arms any better? When are you going to get the treatment the Mayor promised?"

Liv rubbed her face with her hands.

"My arms are still painful. Legs too. Though the treatment was never really..."

She took a large sip of the ersatz whisky and refilled. She seemed to fade into another part of her mind, somewhere unsettled, newly wired.

"It was never something he'd planned to follow up on. I've known that for a while now. I should've told you."

"But he swore to me he'd arrange it?" Bjørn almost shouted.

"I know. Did you believe it though?"

"Yes. I..."

He felt his chair going soft beneath him, like the table was sagging away under his arms.

" Now, I've got a... I don't know." She shook her head.

"What?"

"Ah, it's probably nothing. I'm just a little... uneasy."

She looked scared suddenly, like he'd never seen her before.

"About what?"

"I don't know. Just a bit anxious."

Bjørn felt his pulse in his thighs, his vision growing narrow. He leant forward.

"You don't know why?"

"No. Not really. It's. I don't know. It's like I've got this pressure down here somewhere."

She touched her upper abdomen with both hands.

"Like stress you mean?"

"Yeah, maybe. That's probably it."

A clutching pain appeared in Bjørn's neck and jaw.

"Don't worry. It's probably nothing. I'm just..."

She smiled at him and reached out an arm and touched his cheek.

"I'm just not seeing an end to it. That's all. That's what's making me feel worried I guess. It's psychosomatic."

She looked out the window.

"I've started missing home too."

She said it matter-of-factly, still looking out the small snow-free opening at the top of the floor-to-ceiling window.

Her eyes watered.

"Oh," Bjørn said.

His stomach and intestines were bunching up on him, contents liquefying, threatening uncontrolled evacuation. It was his fault. His string of useless fuckups, stretching back into adolescence, his inability to keep things simple. He'd brought her to this wobbling IKEA table. At this stage in her life. Her golden years. To help him? When she should've been home with her husband Odin, deep under eiderdown, snug, farting the night away. Working out her retirement. Going to the gym to soak in the Jacuzzi. Reading her favourite novels again, in front of the fire, sipping red-wine, planning her old age in peace, hoping for grandchildren.

He leant forward and rested his hand on hers. It felt awkward. Like he was going through the motions. Pretending. Even though he really was worried and wanted to show it. Her hand felt so foreign under his, so feminine. He realised he'd never comforted her before. She pulled it back.

He felt confused.

"What do you want me to do?" he said, trying not to raise his voice.

"Fly you home tomorrow?"

"Don't raise your voice. Don't make it harder."

He could swear she was already slurring her words. He hated that. He felt his stubbornness coming awake, butting and moving inside him, a ball of fat bobbing in the acid of his stomach, something he couldn't really digest or puke up. It was accusing him of making it grow so intolerable.

His mother shook her head quietly, looking at him. She got to her feet with a lot of pain. She walked slowly past him and stopped for a few seconds. Then she walked into the kitchen and put her tumbler down in the sink. He heard the way the glass scraped against the metal. She was crying.

"Why are you crying Liv?"

She didn't answer him.

"What is it? What did I say?"

She cried painfully.

"Don't," she said.

"Don't what?" he almost shouted.

"Don't shout."

In a way he felt betrayed. Like he'd been promised to go somewhere but had suddenly been left behind. The others gone. The room felt stupidly implicated. Its dull mediocrity. The fact that this was where he was. Where he'd ended up. The unremarkable quality of everything around him. The thick layer of dust on the floor. The fucking surfboard attached to the ceiling. When would somebody get rid of that ridiculous thing? He felt childish. He felt angry with himself for being so stubborn. He couldn't handle hearing his mother cry.

He looked out the window, out at the falling snow, its gazillion individual flakes undistinguishable, always falling. He sighed and dropped his palms heavy on the table. He turned to look at his mother.

"Goodnight Bjørn."

She walked off, her upper body trembling. He could hear her going to the bathroom, running the tap. He assumed she brushed her teeth. Then it was quiet for a while until the toilet flushed.

He walked out into the hallway.

The bathroom was empty. The light off. The cistern was almost done refilling. In the darkness he walked up to his old room's door. He knocked and waited a bit before he opened it.

His mother looked at him, her uncoiffed head sticking out at the far end of the duvet. The reading light was on. Her eyes were red.

"Come here," she said.

He walked over and sat down on the bed, feeling the weight of her body against his right thigh, smelling her night-cream.

"It'll be alright. You know that?"

"I know," he whispered.

The pressure in his throat felt devastating. He closed his eyes and his tears dropped onto the floral pattern of the duvet-cover.

"So so, my son."

She took his hands and held them tight.

"We'll be fine you know. We'll be fine. I'm sorry about earlier."

"Me too," he said, "It's just that I feel I've..."

"... let me down?"

"Yes."

"No. You could never do that. It's impossible. You're my boy. You couldn't let me down."

"But..."

"No. You couldn't. You shouldn't think that way. You were always so sensitive, since you were a child. Let it go Bjørn. Things happen. It wasn't your fault. You didn't sign that contract, did you? It wasn't you who sold the equipment? You didn't make it snow?"

"I know."

"So then? You still let it get to you? You shouldn't."

"I know."

"It's not up to us."

"I know."

She stroked his hands and wet cheeks.

"We'll find a way, OK?"

"OK."

"Goodnight. I'll see you in the morning."

She pulled him towards her and gave him a long hug.

/>

<the_body_rebellious

The day after, Liv woke up and felt she couldn't really get
out of bed, but nonetheless broke herself free from the warm
duvet and walked painfully into the small apartment's
mouldy bathroom to have her customary morning shower.
Trying to turn on the water her right hand felt like it froze
solid around the temperature control. She used her left
hand to ply the fingers open. The sparse cold water was
trickling over her aching body. For every small movement
she made with her feet in the bathtub she had the sensation
of walking on a large and loose sack of potato-flour. It was
as if her body below her breasts was no longer a part of her,
aching in a dull foreign language. She turned off the water
with the same stiff fingers and dried herself briefly with a
lot of pain. She avoided looking into the steam-free mirror,

wrapped the towel around her, opened the bathroom door, and with a trail of water dripping from her feet, walked slowly back to her borrowed bedroom.

She closed the door behind her and stood for a second looking at the things in her son's room. His small non-descript IKEA desk, his IKEA wardrobe, his few framed posters, the Victorinox knife his father (and her ex-husband) had given him for his 10th birthday, placed on his IKEA bedside table. She sighed and felt the strangeness of her body again. It felt like something had decided to start a rebellion in each muscle. For every movement she made this insurgent force mounted an immediate counter-attack. She'd been in pain before, constantly, for years, but this was something else, this was acute, paralysing.

Still she managed to get dressed, and wearing her all-weather outfit, her lightweight water-repellent GORE-TEX trousers, her three super-breathable layers of sports underwear, her famous skier-brand woollen socks, she walked slowly into the kitchen-cum-living-room where Bjørn was sitting at the wobbly dinner table, his head in his hands, a mug of instant coffee in front of him.

Liv saw his face turn worried as she entered. She tried to smile.

"Are you OK Mamma? You look..."

"Yeah, I don't know, this morning."

She sighed and tried to sit down on the low stool, but gave up and leant against the wall, unsteady.

Bjørn jumped up and came around the table and held her by the shoulders and helped her to his chair. She sat down and tears were coming down her cheeks. She clenched her jaws and tried to breathe slowly through her nose.

"What is it Mamma?"

Liv couldn't answer. She drew her breath loudly through her mouth and then exhaled, loudly again, her fingers and arms trembling, her shoulders trembling. Bjørn could feel it as he held his hands there.

"What is it Mamma?"

She took a deep breath and then doubled over from a sudden pain in her abdomen.

"Mamma!" Bjørn cried.

She didn't reply.

"Mamma," he whispered, "what's the matter?"

"I don't know, I..."

She crouched over again, reacting to another burst of pain, and let out an agonising moan.

"Help me. Lie. Down."

Bjørn led her over to the beanbag where she let go of his arms and lay down, slowly curling up on her side, facing away, clutching the upper part of her stomach, still trembling. She didn't say anything but lay there clenching

and unclenching her jaw for every shock of pain that past
through her. She was looking towards the floor-to-ceiling
windows.

/>

<skiing_alone

Bjørn felt a hollowness come over him he'd never felt before. For the first time in his life he understood what it meant to be really sad. No matter what he tried to think about he couldn't shake it. Maybe his mother would be fine this time, it was likely, the doctors said, but soon enough she would be gone. He was surprised by how deeply he grieved already for what would come. He could imagine his mother being dead. He thought about never hearing her voice again.

He skied in amongst the skyscrapers on Canada Square in heavy snow. He stopped in front of the HSBC headquarters and saw his own reflection in the giant windows, the ones still intact. He shouted as loudly as he could, looking at himself as he did so. He saw his mouth open and his tongue in the middle of it. He saw his red eyes and his forlorn expression. The shout had no echo in the muffling snow. He shouted again, and he looked at himself shouting, and he saw the same open mouth and the same sad eyes. The sound was immediately gone. His eyes looked so childish in their red swollenness. His lower lip quivering like it had done when he was a boy. He looked at himself. He felt he was dissolving in front of his eyes. His blue hat floated in mid-air. His red anorak with the snow settling on it. His grey gloves hanging motionless by his thighs. His skis' tracks were covering over.

How long had he been standing there?

It was getting dark, and the streetlights were out. He looked at his own eyes as best he could between the snowflakes. He bore into the eyes in the reflection, thinking he had to be in there somewhere. He looked at his own gaze and became more and more strange to himself. He opened his mouth and mimed the word mamma with his lips. He saw himself crying and felt the tightness in his chest and throat. Then he looked away.

But instead of going home he pushed on. He didn't know where to. He wasn't even very conscious of moving. He strained his muscles and his breath to the point where his mind started going blank. He fell into a numbing rhythm, each skating stroke of the skis followed by a hard push with both poles. After a while the snow on the ground became so deep he had to change tack. He was inelegantly ploughing through the heavy mass up to his thighs, his skis catching each other, his poles sinking in too deep. He got warm and started sweating. The salty liquid seeped into his eyes and his mouth. He passed a multitude of looted off-licences, neighbourhood butchers, Costcutters, Tesco Expresses, Tennessee Fried Chickens, Co-Ops, abandoned post offices. He worked so hard he started feeling tingles down his upper back, the shivers extending down his arms and up his scalp. Around him the millions of falling snowflakes fell quietly. Densely. With no interruption. They settled on his hat, his shoulders, they melted on his thighs and made his gloves soggy. His legs started trembling.

He came to a halt on a wide open plain. Panting heavily he turned around. Through the snowflakes he thought he saw a dim line of something darker far behind him, spotted with a few lights here and there. He thought he saw smoke rising from multiple points along the line, but he couldn't be sure, his eyes were so tired. Catching his breath he felt for a moment absolutely at one with his body. The violent dragging in and pushing out of air from his lungs felt like it moved his consciousness from his head to just below his ribs, and from there it felt like his whole body became aware, his trembling legs and thighs, his stiffening arms, the tingles along his spine, the skin of his scalp, his toes filling and emptying with freshly oxygenated blood, his grip around the poles slowly loosening. He thought he felt a moment of bliss. He felt a smile stiffening on his face.

Then he felt dizzy and vomit-sick, and his vision grew more and more constricted. Small bursts of light appeared and immediately faded in front of his eyes. He became afraid, thinking that he might die if he passed out and fell over in the snow. He thought about how selfish he'd been, heading off like this. He thought about how sad his mother would be. He said the word mamma out loud, several times. Then he felt an overpowering tiredness.

[memetic error: possible scrambled file]

He saw a group of people round a conference table. They weren't particularly well-dressed, though their hair looked neatly styled. A man in his late thirties was standing in front of a large whiteboard, a felt-tip marker in his right hand. He was looking at the group of people seated at the table, in a semi-circle facing him. A woman of about twenty-eight was talking energetically, gesticulating in a way Bjørn realised he found very elegant, sexy. The man with the felt-tip marker listened and looked at her, before he turned to the whiteboard and wrote down the words collaboration and individual. Then a young-looking man at the table, almost a boy, Bjørn thought, said something witty and everyone laughed, and the man with the felt-tip pen clapped his hands while smiling, still holding the pen, and noted the word responsibility on the whiteboard. Then for a while the group seemed to become engaged in debate, verging on a quarrel, and the man with the felt-tip pen was struggling to keep their attention, though he managed to do so eventually by tapping the back of his pen loudly on the whiteboard. He started addressing the group in a forceful manner, all the while pointing to words he'd written on the board and drawing lines and arrows and simple diagrams. He ended his performance by wiping a space clean and filling it with two questions in capital letters:

CAN WE RELY ON INDIVIDUAL KINDNESS?
HOW DO WE DEVELOP A COLLECTIVE STRATEGY?

Bjørn felt he recognised the people in the room. But he couldn't put names to faces, nor actually see their features that clearly. He saw them each take a picture of the whiteboard with their mobile phones, then leave the conference room and head for a spacious balcony overlooking a river flowing calmly through a redeveloped harbour area. The old cranes were still towering in place. A few sea gulls took off into the mid-day sky. In the distance a train was moving fast but made no sound. Someone brought out a tray filled with small espresso cups, and everyone started sipping coffee. They looked happy, Bjørn thought, kind to each other. He felt an urge to be a part of their group.

But he moved up into the air and floated down on the other side of the building. He saw men and women running away from an intense red blaze, covering their mouths, blood running down their faces. Advertising signs lay shattered everywhere in their paths. He heard sirens and saw a troop of police firing machine-guns before retreating behind a barricade. A group of about twelve indistinguishable individuals ran away in the opposite direction, each holding something he couldn't see what was. Night fell fast. He thought he'd seen the same scene an infinite number of times. All his life. It was stuck on a loop. The smoke billowing up from an eternal fire. Only the victim's skin colour and hair-style and clothes changed for every re-run.

The scene made him angry and disappointed. As if someone had betrayed him personally. Insulted him. Had ignored his advice. Taken off without paying the bill. It also made him feel he'd forgotten to do something. Something important he couldn't think of. Though it felt like it had to do with not preparing well enough. That he was showing up to give a lecture without his notes.

Suddenly he felt pulled back in time. Someone had taken hold of his shoulders and had jerked him backwards, making him fall with no way of catching himself or seeing what was behind him.

He was back in school and was explaining to his maths teacher why he'd been absent from class all year. He realised he'd not even thought of going to this essential class, and was now faced with an exam he had no way of passing. The teacher would not hear his excuses. Bjørn felt himself pathetically breaking down in tears, pleading and begging the man to give him another chance. His total neglect of the class for a whole year felt like an open hole in his chest, a character-weakness he could no longer hide, the teacher's reproach justified. He walked out of the schoolyard, his head lowered, trying to cover up the hole in his chest with his backpack.

He walked into a large farmyard. It was bright daylight again, but overcast, so he couldn't see the sun. The farm was an old, traditionally built, Norwegian farm. The colour of the barn was the deep red he remembered having seen many times. The farmhouse was a newly painted white, the smell of which mixed wonderfully with the smell of fresh sawdust. He felt relief at being in such a familiar setting, as if he'd finally chanced upon his way home again. The green tall trees either side of the farm's two buildings gave him a sense of great pleasure, their branches undulating quietly in a breeze he couldn't directly feel.

As he walked around the back of the barn he came to a fenced-in area holding an almost infinite number of free-ranging hens. Some of the hens walked back and forth pecking at seeds in the dust. Others stood still just looking around with the familiar jerky movement of the head that chicken have. He recognised this movement and laughed to himself. He remembered having seen it as a child and found it funny. He made a loud chicken noise: bock, bock, bock, bock, bock, baawwwwgk.

He realised the farmer had been observing him since he'd turned the corner. Bjørn thought he must have seen him laugh too, that he must've heard him make the silly chicken noise. Deeply embarrassed Bjørn looked at him. He was a man in his early thirties, with a tightly cropped head of blond hair, a pair of green and yellow industrial overalls loosely tied around his waist. He wore a black t-shirt with the word Slayer printed on it. It was the name of a heavy-metal band, Bjørn remembered. The man held an axe in his right hand. To his left stood a well-worn chopping block made from the lower trunk of a birch tree. Leading up to it, forming a long irregular line, stood thousands of hens, their heads lowered, pecking feathers from the one in front, each one kicking dust backwards, into the eyes of the one behind. As they walked towards the farmer, who picked them up and chopped their heads off, the hens kept laying eggs and kept kicking these backwards as they fell to the ground.

Bjørn felt as if his arms and legs had fallen asleep and were now waking up, prickling and itching. He wanted to document what he was seeing. Put it on tape. Show the world what he'd discovered. But he couldn't move. Instead the slaughter-scene faded slowly into a whiteness below him. And as though he was released from a spell he felt he was slowly surfacing from deep water and rejoiced at the resulting loss of pressure and his ability to breathe again.

He stood in a field of yellow waving crops. A strong light shone from over a mountain range far away. He looked up and saw swallows circling so far above he could really only see them by squinting. The sky was the kind of blue he'd only seen in nature documentaries. But he knew this was real. There was a sky like this. A way of seeing it.

He turned and saw a group of men and women beside him, maybe ten or eleven. They were adults in their thirties, forties and fifties. They were a team of biologists. Their well-trained bodies formed beautiful silhouettes against the strong light rising above the distant mountain range. Following them he saw that each one carried a cut-off water bottle filled with a mixture of earth, straw and moss. They walked quietly, spread out from each other with what looked like an agreed distance. There was something dignified about them. Something solid and balanced. A calmness. At a signal from one of the elder women at the front they all stopped and bent over, parting the yellow crops, proceeding to carefully empty the contents of their water bottle onto the ground. Bjørn approached one of the women at the back of the group and kneeled down to see what she was placing on the ground. It was darker and cooler there, so low to the earth, between the thick stems of the crop. It smelled raw and invigorating. He looked closer. Inside the deposited earth and moss he could see a small spider, red and black, a Ladybird, crawling away into the dust, hiding from them. The female biologist rose and walked quietly on. She took out another cut-off water bottle from her backpack and removed a layer of cling-film from the top. Bjørn saw the team adjusting their agreed distance from each other as they walked away from him. Then they stopped again and went through the same procedure he'd just witnessed, carefully laying down the spiders on the ground.

He turned around. He looked towards the West, with the strong light behind him. It started warming his back. Far away towards the end of the slightly declining plain, approaching another distant mountain range, he saw a long row of combine harvesters moving towards him. The machines were producing an enormous cloud of dust. Bjørn stood still among the yellow crops, watching the machines steadily moving forward. As they came closer and closer he could hear the rising roar of their engines. He turned back to see if he could see the biologists. But the bright light rising above the mountains ahead was so intense he couldn't see them anymore.

/>

<it_knew_it_was_over

High above the city the Awareness felt a fast shifting coming on. A change. A tug downwards. It hovered effortlessly, still allowed to observe. It felt like a piñata somehow, twitching and ruffling with paper-skin. The place was familiar. It recognised everything. All of it. From the point of view of the Awareness the falling snow looked like weightless floating shavings of wood. The light was an even afternoon light. Everything was perfectly knowable. Everything was what it was. There were no surprises. The frame of reference was vibrating. It was the basic vibration of matter, the standing waves and oscillations of background radiation. The Awareness experienced a light melancholy. It sensed a discussion taking place relating to itself. Time was not linear. Everything was laid out like products in a supermarket, notions, tastes, memories, faces, words, sentences. They could be seen in one glance. Words and sentences glowed and vibrated. The people sucked words into themselves. The words seemed to either help or harm them. They behaved like elemental particles. Reacted. Combusted. They changed. The Awareness sensed that the power of words and sentences was underestimated by the people in this building.

The building was covered with metres of heavy snow. It felt a slight shift again, without much change in time and perception of place. A large window was lit up, seen from the outside. The light shone through the snow that had compacted against the pane and the frame. Six people were in the room. Lamps were placed on the floor, candles on the few elevated surfaces. The young woman who had just arrived was hugging another older woman. The Awareness knew who it was. It was Alice, the Dane's girlfriend. Every particle had millions of shadow particles. The light in the room held a multitude of darkness. They were one, the light and the darkness. The sun's rays dispersed through the thick clouds and the falling snow. Around single specks of dust, ice-crystals formed. And formed. And formed. A song was playing: The Power of Love, by Jennifer Rush. The people sat down around the familiar living-room table, really a large desk from IKEA. Liv, the oldest woman in the room, was humming along to the song, in her mind. The song arrived in waves. She was not really paying attention. She was deeply sad. She'd lost her son that day. The Dane, who'd also just arrived, was crying. They drank coffee and tried to comfort each other. The Mayor had the taste of wood in his buttocks. His hips were cramped and needed a stretch. He was tired too, and worried. Sitting alone. Nobody talked to him. His phone's battery was dead. The Awareness knew this, knew it all, as it heard the ruffling of its own piñata skin, twitching pathetically, a paper-doll conductor. An effigy. It was carrying its duvet around, the Awareness was. Some sort of toga-party look. Undignified. It felt sad. Then it felt another tug down. Inwards. A pull towards the people in this room. A sweet longing. The Awareness' edges felt like fur, like animal fur. It knew the secrets now. Hearing them talk like this made it burn all over, with an urge to start again.

Rumbling from machinery in the distance increased. Millions of people pulled curtains aside, shivered, looked out their windows, saw the metres and metres of snow on the ground, weighing down the antennas, filling up satellite dishes, a frozen heavy porridge.

The Awareness felt another pull in, towards the large window, as if its nose was squeezing up against it, pulled through the layers of snow. There was still some sweetness left. Still an attachment. The windsurf board hung from the ceiling. The makeshift TV stood in the corner. The Rowena kettle. The extra bicycle tires, for summer-use. The giant beanbag.

Then it felt the pull slackening. It floated upwards.

The neighbours looked out their windows with tired eyes. Sugar was dissolved into cups of tea. What was left of milk was added. Heaters were turned up. More layers were dug out of cupboards and closets. Still there was someone talking in the lit-up room of six: the Dane, his girlfriend Alice, Bjørn's mother Liv, Kirsty, the Mayor. The Awareness felt itself lifting upwards. Then came a giant dumper, skidding around the corner. It pulled up and a huge metal ball jumped out, tugging on a tall dark man, who slowly climbed down the ladder from the cab, balancing several trays of sweets in both hands. He buzzed and entered. The Awareness knew him.

/>

Kweku told everyone to please have some coffee and cake and to find a seat, if possible. Liv tapped her teaspoon on her mug and got to her feet.

"Thank you for coming, friends."

Her voice was trembling. She took a deep breath and looked down at Kirsty, seated on her right. The room was warm and steam had started covering the insides of the floor-to-ceiling windows.

"Today we could stop searching for my Bjørn. Kweku found him in a field past Ilford."

She turned to look at Kweku and smiled. Both were crying. She dried her eyes and turned around again.

"Many months ago I spoke to you. After we had seen the initial damage the snow had done. I told you I wanted us to look for the best in us. Do you remember? To make sure we did not give up. That we had to do our best. I told you I believed there was something good about us."

Everyone around the room and table nodded, even the Mayor.

"I said we should save something about our way of life. For future generations. I do not know if I believed it. I do not know anymore. I hope I did. I have always been good at seeing the positive side. But it feels so long ago now, the months since, like a lifetime. Like it was not me."

She pulled in some snot and took a shallow breath.

"Bjørn, my son, was alive then. We were together."

She rested her right hand on Kirsty's shoulder.

"I felt I could do it. This job. Tackle the snow. To see if we could find a way out of this."

She nodded towards the steamy floor-to-ceiling windows, completely covered in snow. They all looked that way too, as if they tried to see through to some older version of something they didn't really know what was, something they'd perhaps never really known, but still somehow had always felt an outline of. A presence.

"But now, I do not know. I miss my Bjørn."

She stopped and closed her eyes, trying to breathe, pulling at some flowing mucus.

"As does Kirsty I know, and Kweku, and all of you who knew him well."

All around the room nodded.

"There was something about Bjørn that made people look forward to being with him. When he was happy he was good company. He made our lives better. I know that is true. He made me laugh. He made me proud. He was not afraid of trying. He was stubborn, as a son of mine would be."

She laughed and they laughed with her and were able to breathe a little deeper. But then she seemed to get lost in thought, her gaze slipping out of focus. Her arms involuntarily moved upwards. She covered her mouth with her hands, her eyes staring into somewhere interior. She found her chair with the back of her knees and sat down, closing her eyes. She heard Kirsty and Kweku asking if she was all right, if she needed to lie down, if she wanted water. She shook her head. Murmuring broke out, quite soothing.

Then she suddenly got up and tapped her mug with the teaspoon and the room went silent.

"I am sorry. I was just thinking about my son."

She steadied herself by leaning down on the wobbly table.

"I know I said I did not know just now. That I was not

sure anymore if something is still worth preserving about us. That future generations should also have a chance to feel what this was like."

She held her arms out.

"I know I told you I was not sure anymore."

She scanned the faces looking at her, trying to meet their eyes, even the Mayor's. She felt she was, against her will, regaining some gritty form of strength, a basic sense and shape inside her that was both familiar and strange, a sense of her own bedrock.

"I do not know what happened to Bjørn. Why he is dead. He went out skiing and did not come back. So many people have died over the last months. Wolfgang too, the young man who used to own this apartment."

The Dane nodded.

"We do not know where it is headed. We never did. Even before it started snowing. If I told you earlier I had lost faith, well, that is how I feel today. But who am I to talk?"

She looked down at the table, took a deep breath and looked up again.

"Something unexpected must have happened to my son. Kweku told me he was smiling when they found him. That he held his arms out. Like a polar explorer."

She looked at Kirsty and took her hand.

"It makes me so sad. That is all I know. I will not see him again."

Her own words were sapping her strength. She looked at the Dane, the Mayor, Alice, Kweku and Kirsty. She let her eyes try to find the core in theirs, to try to let them truly know her. Then she looked up and tried to imagine the snowstorm on the other side of the snow-covered windows.

/>

www.ingramcontent.com/pod-product-compliance
Lightning Source LLC
Chambersburg PA
CBHW021225060726

47590CB00005B/1639